I flung the car door open, grabbed my bag and jumped out. I was furious and I was upset. I hadn't forgotten Tanya's thoughtless remarks about how 'lucky' I was. Well, at the moment I felt like the unluckiest girl in the whole world...

For Robert, a fellow football fan

www.thebeautifulgamebooks.co.uk

ORCHARD BOOKS
338 Euston Road, London NW1 3BH
Orchard Books Australia
Level 17/207 Kent Street, Sydney, NSW 2000

First published in 2010 by Orchard Books

ISBN 978 1 40830 422 8

A CIP catalogue record for this book is available
from the British Library.

10 9 8 7 6 5 4 3 2 1

Printed in Great Britain

Orchard Books is a division of Hachette Children's Books,
an Hachette UK company.

www.hachette.co.uk

THE BEAUTIFUL GAME

Friends and football – the perfect match

LAUREN'S BEST FRIEND

NARINDER DHAMI

ORCHARD BOOKS

PROLOGUE

'Mum! Come and look!' Lauren yelled excitedly. She kicked off her trainers and slung her hand luggage onto the sofa before rushing across the enormous hotel room. 'This is so cool!'

Lauren slid back the glass doors and stepped out onto the balcony. The sun was baking hot, a burning fireball in the clear, cloudless sky. Below her was a heart-shaped swimming pool, surrounded by palm trees and sun beds. And just beyond that were the crowded beach, shimmering aquamarine sea and glitzy designer shops of Palm Beach, Florida.

'I can't wait to have a swim,' Lauren sighed, leaning her elbows on the balcony rail. 'The plane journey just went on for *ever*. Oh, and, Mum, I *love* that you hired that pink convertible. I'm going to feel like Barbie riding around in that! The girls are going to laugh like crazy when I tell them—'

Lauren stopped suddenly as she realised that she was talking to herself because her mum hadn't joined her on the balcony. She ducked back into the hotel room and scowled as she saw her mother sitting on the four-poster bed, mobile phone clamped to her ear.

'Sorry, honey,' Mum whispered to Lauren. 'A few problems back home in the office I need to deal with.'

'I want to go for a swim,' Lauren said in a sulky voice. She didn't care if the person on the other end heard her, either. This was supposed to be a *holiday*, Lauren thought crossly. They'd only been in Florida for five minutes and already her mother's office had been in touch!

'Just a moment.' Mrs Bell covered the mouthpiece of the phone and then smiled at Lauren. 'You have a shower to freshen up, sweetie, and then go on down to the pool. I'll be finished in a little while.'

I've heard THAT one before, Lauren thought bitterly, rolling her eyes. She grabbed her neon-pink bikini, matching beach towel and sequined flip-flops from her suitcase, and flounced into the marble bathroom. It was always the same with her mum and dad. Work, work, work. Her dad hadn't even managed to find the time to come on holiday with them. As far as Lauren's parents were concerned, their jobs were more important than everything else.

Even more important than me, Lauren thought as she turned on the shower. And she had to blink several times to stop the tears in her eyes from falling.

CHAPTER ONE

One minute I was running along with the ball at my feet. The next minute, I was rolling around on the grass, all the breath knocked out of me, clutching my sore ankle.

'Ouch!' I groaned, as the whistle blew. 'Ref, *do* something will you?'

'Oh, stop whining,' the Melfield United defender, Lily Scott, muttered as she walked away. 'I didn't hurt you *that* much.'

Well, maybe she didn't, but that wasn't the point, was it? It was about the *tenth* time she'd tackled me so clumsily during the game, and I'd had enough.

I'm a nice person usually, honest. But sometimes... Well, I don't know what happens, but my blood starts to boil and I get this red mist in front of my eyes and I lose my temper in a big way and then I just don't *care*.

Which was exactly how I was feeling right now. Fuming, I jumped to my feet and raced after Lily.

'Lauren!' Jasmin shouted from behind me. '*Milkshake!*'

I slowed down and glanced round. Jasmin, Hannah and Grace were all running towards me, screaming, '*Milkshake! Milkshake!*'

'Big, frothy, strawberry MILKSHAKE!' Katy yelled at me from defence. Meanwhile Georgie, our goalie, was jumping up and down in the box, miming slurping milkshake through a straw.

The referee and the Melfield United players were staring at us in bewilderment. Even the rest of our team-mates were watching, open-mouthed, and so were the groups of parents standing around on the touchline. But I stopped dead and started giggling. I guess you're probably thinking that our team, the Springhill Stars, are as nutty as a bar of fruit and nut chocolate by now! But we're not *really*.

I guess it all started when our coach Freya chose

the six of us – that's me, Jasmin, Grace, Hannah, Georgie and Katy – to go on an intensive football course during the first week of the Easter holidays. I didn't know the others that well before then, although Jasmin and I had been to the same primary school. Hannah and Katy were both new to the team, so I didn't know them at *all*. Anyway, during the week the course lasted, the six of us became mates. Ooh, that sounds so easy, doesn't it? Well, it wasn't! We had some mega ups and downs because we're all such big characters (and that's a nice way of putting it). We made up though, but then it all nearly fell to bits again because I played a silly joke on Hannah. I felt *so* bad about it afterwards, and I really thought that was *it*. The end of our friendship. But to cut a long story short, we decided to have our very own special word to say when we thought someone was getting angry and they ought to cool it. You've guessed it! *Milkshake!*

'OK, you mad, crazy people,' I said, holding up my hands. 'I give in.'

'It worked!' Jasmin squealed in delight. 'We're winning 2–1, Lauren, and you *mustn't* get sent off now.'

'You're a star.' Grace patted me on the back.

'Now just calm down and count to ten and *breathe*.'

'Lily's really giving you a hard time, Lauren,' Hannah chimed in. 'But you're doing brilliantly, and there's only five minutes left to go.'

'Sorry to interrupt,' the ref called grumpily, 'but can we finish the game, please?'

As Hannah ran to get the ball to take our free-kick, both Georgie and Katy gave me a double-thumbs-up from the other end of the pitch. I felt quite proud of myself. For once, I'd managed to control my hot temper, thanks to the other girls. But if Lily Scott hacked me down again, there was still every chance that I might just do something I'd regret the second after it happened!

I sighed as Hannah booted the ball to Grace. Whatever the others said, I'd had a rubbish game, and actually it wasn't just because of Lily Scott's terrible tackling. I was feeling all *bleurgh* at the moment, and I wasn't really sure why...

I suppose a bit of it was because we'd started back at school this week after the end of the Easter holidays. But I think it was mostly because the Stars had gone all out for promotion to the next league this year, but we hadn't made it. We only had four matches left until the end of the season, and we were completely out of the running. I was *so* disappointed. Oh, and Mum and I had gone to Florida last week on holiday, which had been a *total* disaster—

'Lauren!'

I jumped and realised, too late, that Emily Barnard had just passed the ball to me. Helplessly I watched it spin out of play for a throw-in to Melfield.

'Sorry,' I called back. Emily shrugged and rolled her eyes, looking a bit put out.

'You're half-asleep, Lauren,' Georgie called from our goalmouth. Grace is our captain, but Georgie likes to yell at us all the time. She says it keeps us on our toes. 'Wakey, wakey!'

Feeling guilty, I glanced over at Freya, who was standing on the touchline. She frowned at me, shook her head and tapped her watch. I knew what that look meant. *Only a few minutes to go – concentrate!!!*

'You need a kick up the backside, Lauren Bell,' I muttered to myself, 'and I'm giving you one right now!'

I was usually a bit disappointed whenever a match ended, especially when it was a sunny, blue-sky kind of morning like today, but I was very relieved to hear the final whistle. I'd managed not to make any more mistakes (basically because I'd only touched the ball once or twice during the last few minutes anyway), and we held on to our lead to win.

'Thanks for a good game, Lauren,' Lily Scott said, coming over to slap me on the back as the spectators applauded.

'You too, Lily,' I replied, resisting the overwhelming urge to kick her on both ankles.

'Ooh, I know exactly what you're thinking, Lauren,' Jasmin said, wagging her finger at me as Lily went off with the rest of her team-mates. 'You *so* mustn't do that!'

I grinned at Jasmin and slung my arm across her shoulders. 'OK, I'll be a good girl, I promise.'

'How long will *that* last, Lauren?' Grace teased. She pulled out her pink hair elastic and let her straight, shiny blonde hair cascade down over her shoulders.

'Grace, how do you always manage to look so gorgeous after a match?' Hannah asked enviously, coming to join us as we strolled off towards the changing-rooms. 'I just *know* my hair's sweaty and sticking up, and that my face is as red as a tomato.'

'Oh, but Lauren's the glamorous one at the

moment,' Grace added, smiling at me. 'Look at you, all brown and healthy after your fab holiday.'

I smiled back, but said nothing. I hadn't told the others just how *not* fab my holiday had been. Mum had spent most of the week on her phone and laptop, sorting out work problems. So we'd hardly used the pink convertible she'd hired, and I'd spent most of the time sitting by the pool on my own. I'd got a great tan, but I was bored out of my *skull*. I'd probably gone a bit over the top, though, boasting to the other girls about the wonderful time I'd had. I don't know why. I guess I just didn't want them to feel sorry for me...

Suddenly I felt someone's hands on my shoulders and then I almost collapsed under the weight of that someone jumping onto my back.

'Way to go, Lauren!' Georgie crowed loudly in my ear. She and Katy had come up behind us.

'Thanks, Georgie, but are you trying to kill me?' I groaned, shoving her off. 'You're twice as big as I am!'

Georgie laughed. 'That Lily Scott was really trying it on, Lauren.' She took off her baseball cap and shook out her amazing wild black hair. 'You did good, girl.'

Meanwhile, Katy linked arms with me and gave me a squeeze.

'You handled that brilliantly, Lauren,' she said. 'Good for you.'

I guess Katy's probably the quietest and most reserved of all of us (although she has her moments, believe me!). But when you see that serious look in her big brown eyes, you know she means every word she's saying.

'Thanks,' I said, feeling a lump suddenly pop into my throat. All this love and stuff from the others was really getting to me in a big way just now. Help! What *was* the matter with me?

'Another win then, girls.' Freya said with satisfaction as we reached the far touchline. 'Well done, you.'

'Yeah, shame we had such a bad start to the season,' I sighed. 'We might have had a chance for promotion otherwise—'

'Don't look backwards, Lauren, there's no point,' Freya broke in briskly. 'A good run now will give us all confidence for the beginning of *next* season.' Her piercing blue eyes narrowed as she stared more closely at me. 'Are you OK?'

'Sure.' I shrugged, forcing a smile.

Freya didn't look very convinced, but all she said was, 'Off you go and get changed, then.'

As we trooped off towards the changing-rooms, I glanced back at the pitch, checking the crowd. My mum had dropped me off just before the game and she'd apologised and said that she had to pop to the office in the designer fashion store where she works. She'd promised to be back for the second half of the match, but the game was now over, and there was still no sign of Mum.

Typical, I thought sulkily. All the other girls had someone at the match, except me – well, apart from Katy. But her parents *never* came, so that wasn't unusual. Grace's and Georgie's dads were there and Jasmin's mum, and *both* of Hannah's parents. I was secretly a bit jealous...

My mum doesn't like footie really, and she's so busy with work, she almost never has time to come and watch me play. She often asks Grace's or Jasmin's parents to give me lifts to matches or to training. I knew my dad enjoyed the games, but the problem was that he was hardly ever at home. Dad runs a software business and he travels all over the world. He was away at the moment again, in Germany.

'Come on, Lauren, cheer up.' Georgie elbowed me in the ribs. 'Forget about Lily Scott and her terrible tackling. You should let all that stuff wash right over you, like I do.'

'Huh, you can talk,' I retorted, giving her a friendly shove. 'You've got a worse temper than me, Georgia Taylor.'

'Hey, did you lot hear that?' Georgie yelled at the others, who were way ahead of us. 'Who's got the worst temper? Me or Lauren?'

'Ooh, let me see now,' Jasmin said in a serious voice. 'Well, it's hard to say, really. But you're much bigger than Lauren, Georgie, and so you're *scarier*.'

'I am, am I?' Georgie pulled a fearsome face and then dashed menacingly towards her. Jasmin gave a scream and vanished through the doors into the changing rooms with Georgie at her heels. Hannah, Grace and Katy burst out laughing, and followed them inside. I had to smile too, even though I was feeling all icky and depressed inside.

We played our matches and had our training sessions at Melfield College, which was a brand-new community college with fantastic facilities including four full-size footie pitches. The changing rooms were fab, too – they were spacious and the floors were clean and there were plenty of wooden benches to sit on and we actually had lockers that *locked*. It was luxury compared to some of the away changing rooms!

I walked in to find that Georgie had cornered Jasmin, who was about half her size, near the lockers and was attempting to tie her up with her own towel. The others were watching, laughing their heads off.

'Georgie, let me *go*!' Jasmin pleaded, almost helpless with giggles as she squirmed to get free. 'I take it all back! Lauren's temper is worse than yours.'

'Oh, thanks a bunch,' I said, pretending to be offended. Actually, I wasn't even sure what the truth was. Georgie has a *flaming* temper and she and I have had some *major* fall-outs on and off the pitch. And even though Georgie's so tall and I'm so teeny-tiny, I'm never scared of her. Because when I get that red mist I told you about, I'm not scared of anyone. Anyway, although Georgie acts a bit hard and cool sometimes, I suspect she's a pussycat underneath it all.

We all began stripping off our kits and dragging our stuff out of the lockers. Three of the other girls in our team, Debs, Emily and Alicia, had changed already and left, shouting goodbyes. Ruby and Jo-Jo were nearly dressed too. I'd better warn you now that we're *always* last!

''Bye, you lot,' called Ruby and Jo-Jo as they left together. 'See you at training next week.'

We all yelled goodbye as we threw on our clothes. Then Grace and I went over to the mirror to apply our mascara and lippy.

'Right!' Jasmin pulled on a pair of hot-pink and lime-striped socks, then looked quizzically at the rest of us. 'Who's going to help me with my jeans, then?'

'What did your last maid die of?' Georgie asked, zipping her sports bag shut.

'It's just that they're a bit tight,' Jasmin explained. She took a pair of skinny black jeans out of her locker and held them up. 'Grace and Katy had to help me get them off when we arrived.'

'Yes, you lot missed all the fun,' Katy said with a grin as she combed her shoulder-length dark hair. 'Grace got hold of one of Jasmin's legs and I had the other, and we pulled for about five minutes before we got the jeans off.'

'They *do* look pretty skinny, Jas,' I observed.

'Here's a thought, Jasmin,' Hannah remarked, 'Why don't you try buying some jeans that actually fit you?'

'Well, they *do* fit me – when I eventually get them on!' Jasmin retorted, sticking her feet into the legs of the jeans.

'Team effort, girls!' Grace said with a wink.

Jasmin stood up with the jeans bunched round her ankles, and we all gathered around her, took hold of the waistband and began yanking the jeans up her legs.

'Right, let's see if we can make it to the knees without any casualties!' Hannah yelled. 'Pull as hard as you can!'

'Ooh, be careful!' Jasmin gasped, as we inched the denim up her shins bit by bit.

'OK, the knees are in sight!' Georgie shouted, 'Onwards and upwards. Looks like the backside might be our next major problem!'

'You cheeky monkey—' Jasmin began indignantly. Then she squealed loudly as a particularly hard yank from Georgie made her lose her balance and she toppled over, almost taking the rest of us with her.

So there we all were in fits of laughter watching

Jasmin trying to get up again with her jeans stuck fast around her knees. You know, I can't tell you how much I already *love* these guys! It's just so great to have good mates on the team again. When I first joined the Stars about five years ago, my then best friends Ashleigh and Lulu joined too. But since then Lulu's left the team, and Ash's family has emigrated to New Zealand. OK, so I have some good mates at my school, Riverton Girls, but none of them like playing football. My two best mates, Flo and Daisy, are into ballet and horses. So I *loved* having my new footie friends to hang out and chill with.

We'd just about got Jasmin zipped safely into her jeans when Freya popped her head around the changing-room door.

'Girls, the parents are getting restless,' she announced. 'Come on, get a move on.' She glanced at me. 'Lauren, your mum said to tell you she's arrived too.'

'Oh, right.' I already knew exactly what Mum would say. *Sorry, darling, I meant to come back for the second half, I really did. But there was just so much to sort out at the office...*

'So what's everyone doing for the rest of the weekend?' Georgie asked as we wandered outside the changing rooms and round the side of the college to the car park at the front, where our parents always waited. It would have been quicker to cut through the college building, but it was always locked up on Saturdays. 'I'm doing the couch potato thing today in front of *Soccer Saturday* with a can of Coke and a Mars bar, and tomorrow I'm going to the leisure-centre pool. I *might* have a fight with one of my brothers too. In fact, I probably will!'

'I'm going shopping with some mates from school,' Grace said.

'My little cousin's having a birthday party this afternoon, and Mum told my Auntie Annie we'd go and help.' Hannah sighed, rolling her eyes theatrically. 'Twenty screaming five-year-olds throwing crisps at each other *and* throwing up because they've had too much jelly and ice cream. Lovely.'

'Well, you have a great time, Hannah,' Katy said with a grin, patting her on the shoulder. 'See you all at training on Tuesday.' And she headed off across the car park.

You might have noticed that Katy didn't answer Georgie's question. She's a bit of a quiet one, our

Katy, and she doesn't give a lot away. The rest of us think there's a bit of a mystery going on, but we like Katy too much to poke our noses in and upset her.

'How about you, Lauren?' Grace asked.

'Yeah, come on, Lauren, make us all jealous, why don't you?' Georgie remarked. She had a bit of a devilish gleam in her dark eyes. 'What're you up to? Flying to Paris in your private jet for dinner at the Ritz?'

'Oh, stop, my sides are splitting,' I retorted, poking my tongue out at her. Georgie's always cracking jokes about how well-off my parents are. I don't mind, most of the time, but it gets to me a bit every so often. I wondered what Georgie and the others would say if they knew the truth about my so-called fabulous weekend – that Dad was away and Mum would probably start work on her laptop as soon as we got home. The most exciting thing that could possibly happen was that Gran might come round for tea...

We all shouted our goodbyes and then peeled off across the large, tree-lined car park in different directions towards our parents' cars. Mum was sitting in her black sports car under the trees, and she was on her phone. No surprise there, then. She smiled at me as I climbed in.

'—and the delivery was meant to arrive two days ago.' Mum mouthed *hi, honey* at me and carried on talking. 'I *know* it's Saturday, but we need to get on to this ASAP—'

Jasmin's mum was parked next to us, and I waved at them as they pulled out of the car park. Then I decided that, as it was such a sunny day, I'd put the car roof down. I reached for the switch and flipped it, and the roof began to collapse down.

Mum shook her head violently at me, but I didn't take any notice. I was feeling rebellious. The roof slid smoothly into the open boot, which then closed itself automatically.

'*Lauren!*' Mum finished her call, snapped her mobile shut and glared at me. Even in her jeans and casual white jacket, she looked immaculate and groomed, like she always did. Her make-up was perfect, and she'd had her nails done and her hair blow-dried yesterday. 'It might be sunny today, but it's too cold to have the roof down—'

'No, it's not,' I muttered sulkily. I was feeling *really* out of sorts by now. 'I'm hot after running around for ages, and I want it open!'

God, I sound so spoilt, don't I? I'm not, really. I don't know why I act like this sometimes…

'OK, fine, but don't blame me if you freeze your socks off.' Looking irritated, Mum slid her dark sunglasses off her blonde hair, the exact same colour as mine, and put them on. 'Sorry I didn't get back for the second half, Lauren,' she went on as she revved the engine. 'I wanted to, but there was just so much work outstanding at the office. I thought that if I stayed, I'd get a head-start for Monday.'

Well, not quite word for word, but pretty much what I thought she'd say. I slumped back on the cream leather upholstery and scowled.

'What's going on with you, then, Miss Sour-Face?' Mum asked, as we headed out of the college car park. 'Did you lose the game?'

'No, we won 2–1,' I replied.

'That's great, darling,' Mum said cheerfully. 'I know how much you're loving hanging out with these new mates of yours. It's good for you to do your own thing and be independent.'

I was silent. Mum and Dad both seemed to think that, because I was nearly twelve, I was happy to get on with stuff on my own. Well, I was. *Sometimes*. But there were other occasions when

I just wished that they could be *there* for me a bit more. I suppose I was lucky that Mum didn't have to stay away for her job, though, unlike Dad. On the very rare occasions that Mum and Dad were away on business at the same time, my gran or Mrs Melvyn, our cleaner, stayed overnight to keep an eye on me. My gran is something else. More about her later!

'By the way, Lauren, I have a surprise for you when we get home.' Mum put her foot down, waving airily at some guy she'd just cut up at the roundabout.

'Great,' I said, but not very enthusiastically. That usually meant that Mum had brought me something from the fashion store. I mean, I *love* clothes, but I have a walk-in wardrobe in my bedroom that's already stuffed with millions of outfits. It would take me *years* to wear them all.

But when the electronic gates swung back and we turned into our big, paved drive, I gave a shout of delight. There was a familiar silver Mercedes parked in front of the house.

'Dad's back!'

'I thought that would please you,' Mum said with a smile. 'He wound up his meetings early and managed to get a seat on another flight.'

I flung open the car door and raced towards the front porch as Mum drove the car into the garage. Impatiently, I fumbled to find my key and open the door. Then I rushed inside the large, square hallway that was flooded with sunshine.

'Dad?' I chucked my bag on the tall dresser and then ran over to the bottom of the sweeping mahogany staircase that went up to the top two storeys of the house. 'Dad, where are you?' I called up the stairs. 'I'm home!'

'Hi, sweetheart, I'm in the conservatory.'

I hurried through the huge cream and chocolate-brown living room, with the big plasma TV screen on the wall, and then into the dining room, where my mum hangs all those *weird* modern art pictures she collects. Beyond the dining room was the enormous glass conservatory filled with squishy sofas and lots of exotic-looking flowers. Don't ask me what they are though, the gardener looks after them all!

'Dad!' I yelled.

Smiling a welcome, Dad dropped his newspaper and stood up. When I ran into his arms, he picked me up and swung me round, like he used to do when

I was six years old. OK, so it wasn't very dignified now I was nearly twelve, but I didn't mind every so often.

'How's my best girl?' Dad asked, kissing the top of my head. Dad has light brown hair and blue eyes, and I suppose he's pretty handsome – for a dad! All my friends at Riverton say he's really *cool*.

'Fine,' I replied happily. 'We won 2–1.'

'Great stuff.' Dad winked at me. 'So now we have *two* things to celebrate.'

I looked puzzled. 'What do you mean?'

Dad glanced at my mum as she walked in. 'You haven't told her yet?'

Mum shook her head. 'I wanted to wait until we were all together,' she replied, a huge smile on her face.

'Tell me what?' I asked.

Dad went over to the mini-fridge in the corner and took out a bottle of champagne. Although I hadn't noticed before, there were three crystal glasses ready on the table.

'You tell her, Alyssa,' Dad said, popping the champagne expertly. 'And you only get a taste of this, mind, Lauren!'

'Will someone *please* tell me what's going on?'

I demanded, a bit moodily, I guess. If it was good news, then why did I feel nervous?

'Oh, Lauren, sweetie, I've just been made head buyer at work!' Mum burst out, her green eyes sparkling with delight. 'Isn't that *fantastic* news?'

'That's fab, Mum! Congratulations.' I really *was* pleased for her. But at the very same time, I couldn't help selfishly wondering how this would affect me...

'It means my job becomes a whole lot more interesting,' Mum went on, glowing with pride as she took a glass of champagne from Dad. 'I get to travel abroad and go to all the major fashion shows to buy clothes for the store: London, Paris, New York, Milan—'

My smile faded. It looked *very* much like I was going to be left on my own even more from now on if Mum was going to be away travelling almost as much as Dad.

'What about me?' I asked in a small voice, shaking my head as Dad offered me a glass with no more than a splash of champagne in the bottom of it.

Mum slid her arm around me immediately. 'Oh, Lauren, you're our first priority, you know that,' she said. 'Your dad and I are going to do our best to make sure that we're not away overnight at the same time. But I'm afraid it's going to be much more likely from now on—'

'I suppose Gran or Mrs Melvyn will be looking after me, as usual,' I muttered, trying not to sound too sulky.

'Actually, no.' Dad topped up his champagne glass. 'We can't expect your gran to be on call all the time, and Mrs Melvyn can only spare a night here and there away from her own family. So your mum and I have already discussed this and come up with another solution.'

'What is it?' I said, frowning.

'We've decided to hire a live-in housekeeper,' Dad went on. 'In fact, we started interviewing as soon as we knew your mum was in line for this job. We've already chosen someone called Tanya, who's very nice and has excellent references, and she'll be moving in at the end of the month—'

'WHAT?' I gasped. I could *not* believe what I was hearing! A live-in housekeeper? A *stranger*? And all this had been going on behind my back for weeks? 'You never said *anything* about this to me!'

'Well, there was no point until we knew whether I'd got the job or not, darling,' Mum replied. 'That's why we're telling you now—'

'You have *got* to be joking!' I broke in. 'I'm not being left alone at home with someone I don't know!'

'Lauren, we wouldn't leave you with just *anybody*,' Mum said sharply. 'Tanya is a qualified nanny, and she's got a lot of experience as a housekeeper—'

'I don't care!' I shouted. Here comes that red mist I warned you about. I was so *mad*, I could hardly get the words out. 'I *don't* care how well-qualified the stupid woman is. This is just about the worst thing that's ever happened to me! You don't care how I feel, and I hate you both!'

I turned and ran out of the conservatory, almost knocking over a tall, pink-flowered plant in its ceramic pot. I was ready to burst into tears of rage and misery, and I was only holding them back with difficulty.

But as I ran up to my bedroom, I knew one thing for sure. I was determined that I was going to try to change my parents' mind. And if I couldn't, then I was going to make the new housekeeper's life *hell*. I'd get rid of her if it was the last thing I did.

CHAPTER TWO

'*Lauren!*'

I almost jumped right out of my skin as Grace yelled my name and clicked her fingers about two centimetres from my nose. It was just over a week later, and the six of us were in Grace's pretty lavender and pink bedroom, sprawled on her bed and on comfy beanbags. We'd spent a rainy Sunday afternoon chatting, listening to music and nosing through Grace's *massive* collection of CDs and make-up, but I kept staring off into space, my mind miles away. When I got home, that new housekeeper – Tanya or whatever her name was –

was coming over to meet me. Mum and Dad had tried to reassure me that everything would be all right, but I wasn't having any of it...

'Oh, sorry, Grace,' I muttered. 'I was just thinking about something.'

'Hard work for you, is it, Lauren, thinking?' Hannah said with a grin as she tried out a dark purple nail varnish on her toes. 'Grace just asked if you wanted to choose the next CD. Seriously, though, are you all right? You haven't said much today.'

'You didn't say much at the game against the Windlesea Warriors yesterday, either,' Jasmin said thoughtfully.

'And you played like you had two left feet,' Georgie added, in her usual direct manner. '*Again.*'

I hesitated. The others were staring at me with concern in their faces.

'Hey, guys, don't worry about me,' I said breezily, pretending to be very interested in flipping through a box of CDs. 'I'm cool, just had a really heavy week at school. I came home on Friday with a heap of homework as high as the Eiffel Tower, and I haven't finished it yet. Sorry, I know I was rubbish yesterday, but at least we won again.'

I hadn't told the girls yet what had happened with

Mum and Dad last Saturday. Don't ask me why, because I could have done with some support. I'd had a *horrible* week since I'd found out about Tanya the Terrible, as I'd nicknamed her. I'd tried every trick in the book to get Mum and Dad to change their minds – tears, sulks, blackmail. I'd even tried asking them *nicely*. Nothing had worked – *nothing*. They just kept saying that they wanted someone trustworthy to look after me in our own home while they were both away, and that Gran and Mrs Melvyn weren't always available and they couldn't rely on them. It was Tanya or nothing.

So why hadn't I told the others yet? Well, we didn't go to the same schools, so it wasn't always easy for us to find time to get together in the week. I was the only one at Riverton – Grace, Hannah, Georgie and Katy went to Greenwood Secondary, and Jasmin to Bramfield Girls'. But I'd seen Georgie, Jasmin and the others at training twice last week, and again at the away match against Windlesea yesterday, so I could have told them *then* what had happened. But I hadn't. It was very difficult to discuss problem stuff when we were training or playing a match. Of course, I could have phoned any of them at any time to talk about it. Or I could have told them today, while we were all hanging out together at Grace's. But, again, I hadn't...

Oh, all *right*. I know I'm making excuses! I'll be honest with you. I think it was because I didn't want the others to feel sorry for me. I was embarrassed because they all seemed to think I was living this kind of fantastic, wealthy lifestyle, a bit like a celebrity, and maybe I was. But they didn't know the price I had to pay for it.

'By the way, Hannah, I've been meaning to ask you...' Grace was sprawled on a purple beanbag, looking gorgeous as usual in khaki cut-offs and a spotless white T-shirt, 'how are you getting on with Olivia at the moment?'

'Oh, you mean *Little-Miss-It's-SO-All-About-Me*.' Hannah pulled a face as she carefully painted her toenails. 'Olivia and I are actually getting on *really* well. By the way, girls, that just means that *one*, we don't speak to each other unless we have to; *two*, we're never alone in the same room; and *three*, we haven't killed each other yet. Result!'

We all laughed. When I first met Hannah a couple of months ago, I thought she was a bit quiet and maybe just a touch *boring*. But she isn't at all. She's got this wicked sense of humour and a way with words that just cracks me up. She's pretty too – she has beautiful, thick brown hair, green eyes and a big, friendly smile – but Hannah would never believe me if I told her that. She thinks her evil half-sister, Olivia, is the good-looking one in the family.

'Sorry, girls, I've got to run.' Katy glanced at her watch, then jumped to her feet. 'I'm looking after my little brother this evening while Mum goes to work. See you at training on Tuesday.'

'See you, Katy,' we all called. Katy waved and went out.

'I'd better warn you, girls, I'm going into nosey mode now,' Jasmin said, flipping the tops off two lipsticks and comparing the colours. 'Katy's always going on about her mum and her brother, but she doesn't talk about her dad much, does she?'

'She's mentioned him a few times,' Georgie said. She looked in the mirror and drew on a fake moustache with Grace's black eye pencil. 'He's definitely around.'

'Georgie!' Grace grabbed the eye pencil from her, but she was giggling along with the rest of us.

'I wonder why none of Katy's family ever comes to our games,' Jasmin went on. 'It's a bit of a mystery, isn't it?'

'Girls, Hannah's dad's here,' Grace's mum called. 'Time to break up the party.'

Hannah rushed to put her socks and trainers on, disastrously smudging her wet toenails, which caused more amusement. Then she left in a flurry of goodbyes, along with Georgie and Jasmin, who were getting a lift with her. I lived in the opposite direction to the others, and Grace's mum had already told my mum that she'd drop me back home.

I thought about Katy again as I put on my pink denim jacket. We didn't know a lot about her, just that she was Polish and that she'd only been in this country for a few years. It was obvious that her family wasn't as well-off as any of ours, either. Not that it mattered. But suddenly I felt a bit ashamed of myself. Katy never complained about not having much, but I had *everything* and I still wasn't happy.

'Come *on*, Lauren,' Grace called from the doorway.

Oh, why haven't I told the others what's going on? I thought regretfully, as I followed Grace along the landing. I'd just missed a fantastic opportunity to confess all. Now it was too late, *again*, all because of my stupid pride...

Get over yourself, Lauren Melissa Bell, I thought crossly.

Grace was halfway down the stairs by now and I had to run to catch up with her. As I crossed the landing, the door of one of the other rooms was ajar, and I saw Gemma, Grace's twin sister, lying on her bed. She was reading a magazine, and the Kennedys' Dalmatian dog, Lewis, was curled up beside her. It was always a bit of a shock when I saw Gemma, because she and Grace looked *exactly* alike, even down to their tall, slim figures and the length of their straight blonde hair.

Lewis raised his black and white spotted head inquisitively as I went past the open door, and his tail began to wag furiously as he saw me. I didn't stop. In fact, I speeded up a bit. I'm not a big doggie fan!

When we got downstairs, Grace's mum was already waiting for us on the driveway in her small silver car.

'Thanks for the lift, Mrs Kennedy,' I said, as we climbed in.

I liked Grace's mum, who was small and fair and very pretty, and Mr Kennedy was great too, always joking around. Grace's parents seemed to be very proud of her, and as far as I could remember, Grace had *always* been brought to matches and training sessions by one or both of her parents. She wasn't like me, I thought enviously, passed around from person to person. It was a bit like a game of Pass the Parcel, and *I* was the parcel...

'Are you sure you're OK, Lauren?' Grace asked, twisting around in the front seat to look at me as we drove off. 'Like Hannah said, you've been very quiet again today.'

'I know.' I managed to laugh fairly convincingly. But my tummy was whirling and churning like a washing-machine because I felt so sick at the thought of meeting Tanya. 'I think I probably talk too much, that's the problem – I must remember to keep my big mouth closed more often in future! Anyway, what about our next match? Do you think we'll beat the Shawcross Swallows?'

I thought I'd managed to change the subject quite successfully as Grace and I chatted about next Saturday's game. But when Mrs Kennedy pulled up outside our drive and I said goodbye, Grace turned to me again.

'Give me a ring if you want a chat, Lauren,' she said casually. 'Any time, you know that.'

'Thanks, Grace,' I mumbled. ''Bye.'

That was just like Grace, I thought as I trudged through the open gates. She looked like a model, blonde and beautiful with long legs, and sometimes she got a lot of bitchy comments from girls on some of the other teams we played. But they didn't know Grace like we did. She was one of the nicest people I'd ever met. Maybe I *should* have told her that I was about to meet Tanya the Terrible…

There was a blue and white Mini parked in front of the porch, and I stared at it resentfully as I rang the bell. My parents had bought it for Tanya so that she could get the shopping and pick me up from school, that kind of thing. Well, if I had my way, Tanya wouldn't be using that car for very long at all…

I rang the bell, keeping my finger on it until a few moments later Mum flung the door open.

'Oh, it's you, Lauren,' she remarked, opening the door wider. 'I thought it was a particularly aggressive double-glazing salesman!' She grinned at me, but I deliberately didn't respond.

'Sorry, I forgot my key,' I mumbled, stony-faced.

Mum's smile faded. 'Come and meet Tanya,' she went on briskly. 'Your gran's here too.' She stared hard at me. 'I hope I don't have to remind you to remember your manners, Lauren?'

'Mum, I'm not four years old,' I retorted, marching inside, chucking my bag down and folding my arms sulkily.

'Are you sure?' Mum asked, raising her eyebrows.

I was about to make some smart retort – which would *definitely* have earned me a right telling-off – when I suddenly spotted two battered red plastic suitcases at the bottom of the stairs.

'What are *those*?' I demanded.

'They're Tanya's,' Mum replied calmly.

'But – you said she wasn't moving in until the end of the month!' I spluttered.

'Darling, there's been a slight change of plan,' Mum replied apologetically. She tried to slip her arm around me, but I pulled away. 'Just come and meet Tanya. I'm sure you'll like her.'

And I'm sure I won't, I thought as I reluctantly followed Mum into the living-room. And what was this *change of plan* that Mum had mentioned? It looked very much like Tanya was moving in immediately. Like, *right now*.

Dad was sitting on one of the big, squashy, cream sofas. My gran was next to him, bending over the tray of tea and biscuits. And there, in a leather armchair, sat Tanya the Terrible, teacup in hand.

'Oh, Lauren, there you are.' Gran jumped up and came to hug me. She's very small and slim and, like my mum, always looks like she's just stepped out of a beauty salon. 'I was getting worried, darling. Your mum said you were supposed to be home half an hour ago.'

'Gran! I was only at Grace's,' I said, not looking once in Tanya's direction. Gran could fuss for England at the Olympics and win gold. 'I had to wait until Mrs Kennedy was ready to give me a lift home.'

'Grace – she's one of your *football* friends, isn't she?' Gran didn't quite shudder in disgust, but she said the word *football* like it was a bad taste in her mouth. Gran absolutely hates me playing for the Stars, and keeps trying to persuade me to give it up and be more of a 'lady', as she puts it. No chance.

I nodded. 'How are you, Gran?' I asked a bit naughtily.

'Well, let me see.' Gran heaved a sigh. 'Where shall I start? My ankles are playing up again, and my doctor said—'

'Mum, darling, can we talk about this later, please?' my mum broke in. I smothered a grin. Gran's the world's most enthusiastic invalid. Ask her how she is, and it's like winding up a clockwork toy – off she goes. Don't get too panicked, though. My gran seems to be as fit as a flea, from what I can make out! 'I'd like to introduce Lauren to Tanya.'

There was that warning note in Mum's voice and I knew I'd have to behave myself. In front of my parents and Gran, anyway. I had other plans for when Tanya and I were on our own...

'Hello, Tanya,' I said, turning to look at her properly for the first time.

Tanya put her cup down on the side table and stood up. She wasn't very tall – in fact, she was quite small and slight, and she had very fine, light blonde hair and big pale-blue eyes, and she didn't look terrible or scary *at all*. That would make my plan to get rid of her a whole lot easier, I thought with satisfaction.

'I'm very pleased to meet you, Lauren,' Tanya said with a smile, but she looked a bit anxious.

Ha! She'd be whole lot more anxious when I got going! She had an accent that reminded me a little of Katy's, and she was very softly-spoken and gentle in her manner. *This would be like taking candy from a baby.*

'Are you from Poland, Tanya?' I asked curiously.

Tanya shook her head. 'No, I am from Slovakia. Your mum says you have a Polish friend?'

'Yes, her name's Katy,' I replied. I'd say just enough to make Mum and Dad think that I was being reasonably friendly, and to get Tanya off her guard.

'Another of your *football* friends, Lauren?' Gran said with a loud sigh. 'I don't know about *you*, Tanya, but I must say I do think that football isn't a *women's* game at all. It's fine for men like that lovely David Beckham, but not for us girls—'

'Lauren, you probably guessed on seeing Tanya's suitcases in the hall that she's moving in with us immediately,' Mum said. 'The reason is...' she hesitated, looking a bit uncomfortable. God, I could *totally* guess what was coming. 'Well, unfortunately both your dad *and* I have to be away on business for a few nights later this week, and so Tanya kindly agreed, at very short notice, to start the job early—'

'Oh, *Mum*!' I burst out. I couldn't help it. 'That's not fair! I'm sure Tanya's very nice.' I had to force the words out. 'But I don't know her at *all*.'

'Lauren, honey, it's only for a couple of days,' Dad said reassuringly, although he looked a bit unhappy too. 'I go on Wednesday afternoon, and your mum goes early on Thursday morning so you'll have time to get to know Tanya before we go. And we'll both be home by Sunday.'

'I'll be popping in every day too,' Gran reassured me.

'And both Auntie Lucy and Auntie Rehana said you can ring them anytime if you're feeling lonely, sweetie,' Dad added, taking my hand and squeezing it. 'It's not an ideal situation, we know that, and your mum and I are determined to make it up to you.'

Well, make it up to me by staying at home, then! That was what I wanted to say, but I didn't. I stared down at my feet, horrified to realise that there were tears trembling on my lashes. Maybe I *should* be able to cope with Mum and Dad going away. My parents certainly seemed to think I was old enough and independent enough. But that just wasn't the way I felt, and I didn't know how to put it into words without making myself look whiny and spoilt and demanding and childish...

'Well, that's all settled, then,' Mum said. But she still sounded a little upset, and I knew she was staring at me, willing me to smile and say I was OK with it. But I wouldn't. *No way.* 'Tanya, let me take you upstairs to the loft room,' Mum went on after a tense silence. 'I showed you around it when you came for your interview, remember? It's very private, and you have lots of space and your own bathroom...'

Mum and Tanya went out, Mum still talking.

'I'll make some more tea.' Gran picked up the tray and promptly handed it straight to Dad. 'You don't mind carrying this into the kitchen, do you, Nathan? It's far too heavy for my weak wrists. Then we can all sit down together with a nice cup of tea and watch the *Antiques Roadshow*.'

Dad winked at me behind Gran's back as she hurried out.

'I don't know if I can stand the excitement,' he said. I didn't smile, and Dad bent his head to stare closely at me.

'Are you OK with all this, sugar?' he asked hesitantly. 'Tanya really *is* very nice—'

'Oh, Dad, I'm fine,' I interrupted him sulkily. 'I'm not a *child*.'

But I *felt* like a child. A little kid whose opinion and feelings didn't matter one bit. Why do parents always ask if you're OK with decisions that they've already made *and* when they've got no intention of changing their minds? I wanted to scream and shout that *no, I wasn't OK with it*, but I'd done that when they'd first told me about Tanya and it hadn't made a single bit of difference, had it?

No, if I was going to get rid of Tanya, I was going to do this *my* way.

I didn't sleep very well that night. Oh, what a surprise. I kept waking up every hour or so, and the first thought that flew into my head was that Tanya the Terrible was in the loft just above my head, lurking there like a giant spider. I hate Monday mornings anyway, and today it was rainy and dark and miserable and when my alarm went off, I just wanted to pull the covers over my head and hide in bed all day.

Gloomily, I dragged myself out from under my warm duvet and put on my Riverton School uniform, or my 'fashion statement' uniform, as Georgie calls it. She's joking, of course. I don't know who decided on the Riverton colour combo, but he or she must have been colour-blind. Emerald-green blazer and jumper, a blue skirt, green and blue stripy tie and – get this – a blue beret. The boys from Notwood High, the secondary school near Riverton, just *love* trying to nick our stupid berets off our heads every chance they get.

For some reason, it took me *ages* to get ready this morning. I couldn't find my favourite pair of black over-the-knee socks, so I tipped the drawer out all over the bed. I found them eventually, but I left all the other socks lying on the crumpled duvet. Well, Tanya could clear it up, couldn't she? She was *supposed* to be the housekeeper.

Then I couldn't find a clean white school shirt in my wardrobe. By this time I almost had steam coming out of my ears like some mad cartoon character. I slid a black camisole on over my bra and stomped downstairs. I'd probably have to iron my own shirt, I thought grumpily as I went to the kitchen. My parents were terrible at getting up in the mornings. I quite often had breakfast on my own while I watched TV and waited for either Mum or Dad to stumble downstairs, bleary-eyed, when it was almost time for them to go to work and drop me off at school on the way. I didn't know if Tanya was up yet or not, and I didn't care.

I flung open the door and came to a dead stop in the entrance. The black, cream and chrome kitchen was warm and brightly lit, and there was a smell of toast and coffee in the air. A radio played softly in the corner. Tanya stood at an ironing board in the middle of the room, a heap of creased clothing beside her.

'Good morning, Lauren,' she said, smiling at me. 'Your mother asked me to have a school shirt ready for you.' She held it out to me, beautifully ironed without a single crease. 'I have made your breakfast too.'

I was too gobsmacked to say anything, so I just took the shirt in silence and slipped it on as I sat at the table. Meanwhile Tanya put the iron down andbustled over to the oven. The next moment she placed two poached eggs and toast in front of me.

'Mrs Bell asked me to cook this for you,' Tanya said. 'She told me it's your favourite. I've been keeping it warm for you.'

I stared down at the plate in front of me. The eggs looked *perfect* – I can't stand them when they're too hard or too soft – and the toast was dark brown but not burnt, just how I liked it.

'I'm not hungry,' I snapped, folding my arms. Secretly, I was *starving*.

Tanya frowned. 'Your mother wants you to have

breakfast, Lauren,' she said firmly. 'So you *must* eat it.'

I hesitated. I wanted to retort that she had no right to tell me what to do. But I knew she'd go straight to Mum, and then I'd be in big trouble. Somehow I had to work out how I was going to annoy Tanya in a way that wasn't going to drop me right in it with my parents...

'Lauren!' There was a sharp edge to Tanya's voice which made me jump. 'I'm asking you to eat your breakfast right now, please.'

We stared at each other in hostile silence. I shrugged and pushed the plate away from me. And for some reason, that *really* wound Tanya up.

'Are you always so stubborn, Lauren?' she burst out furiously, her face flushing bright red. 'There are many girls in the world that would gladly change places with you. Girls who don't have half the things you have. Do you realise how lucky you are?'

I glared right back at her. I didn't know why Tanya had got so upset all of a sudden over a stupid plate of poached eggs, but I wasn't going to let her talk to me like *that*. What did Tanya know about me and my life? *Nothing*. All right, so I lived in a big house and my parents had lots of money and I had loads of stuff, but my mum and dad didn't care about me as much as they cared about their work. So how did that make me lucky?

Before I could say anything, though, I heard my mum's footsteps on the stairs overhead. Her face set, Tanya turned back to her ironing, and I saw my chance. Quick as a flash, I stabbed one of the eggs with my fork, and the yellow yolk spurted out, all over my clean white shirt.

'Oops!' I sighed. 'Oh dear. Now see what I've done.'

Tanya watched me angrily as I undid the shirt, yanked it off and threw it on top of the pile of ironing. My mum came in a few seconds later, wrapped in her pink silk dressing gown.

'Good morning, Tanya. Hello, honey.' Then she clicked her tongue in annoyance as she saw me sitting there in my camisole top. 'Tanya, can you iron a school shirt for Lauren, please? I did ask you yesterday not to forget.'

I kept my eyes wide and innocent as I turned to glance at Tanya. She looked very annoyed, and I thought she might explain to Mum what had happened. But she didn't. Instead she simply nodded and began rummaging through the pile of clothes, looking for another clean shirt. I smiled to myself – OK, it wasn't much, but I'd got the better of Tanya on our very first day. She'd *soon* realise just how much of a handful I could be!

'Sorry, Tanya,' I said, smiling sweetly when Mum had poured two mugs of coffee and gone back upstairs. 'Mum and Dad should have warned you – I'm very high-maintenance. I need a *lot* of looking-after.'

'Thank you for telling me that, Lauren,' Tanya said calmly. 'But I can see for myself that you have been just a little bit spoilt.'

Well! What a cheek! I glared at her.

'But never mind,' Tanya went on, laying out another of my school shirts on the ironing board. 'I'm sure we're going to get along just *fine*.'

There was the hint of a challenge in her voice that I wasn't expecting. But only one of us was going to lose this battle, and it *definitely* wasn't going to be me.

CHAPTER THREE

'So what are you two up to this evening?' I asked my mates Flo and Daisy, as we strolled through the Riverton School gardens towards the gates. 'No, wait – let me guess. You're probably going tearing around the countryside on those horrible, smelly animals that have massive scary teeth at one end, and are always pooing from the other?'

'If you mean are Daisy and I going for a quiet ride through the countryside on our two beautiful, well-behaved horses, Lauren, the answer's *yes*,' Flo retorted with a grin, jamming her beret on top of her long red hair. It was the end of the school day, and pupils were streaming out of the gates towards the cars, waiting to pick them up.

'So what are *you* doing this evening, then, Lauren?' Daisy chimed in. She was tiny and fair, like me, and people sometimes said we looked a little like sisters. 'No, hang on – it's Tuesday, so that means you must be running around a muddy field getting all sweaty and smelly yourself!'

I laughed. 'Yep, got it in one, it's footie training for me tonight, guys.'

Flo shuddered dramatically. 'God, Lauren, I simply don't know *how* you can enjoy playing football. I mean, it's just kicking a ball around for hours on end. How boring is *that*?'

'I'd rather kick a ball around than get bitten on the backside by a hungry horse!' I said, anxiously scanning the road for Mum or Dad's car as we reached the gates. I was a bit worried that if they were both busy, they might have sent Tanya to collect me. Since the school-shirt incident yesterday morning, we had avoided each other. And when I got home from school, Tanya *hadn't* put my socks away or made my bed. Apparently, she'd asked Mum if she should tidy my bedroom and Mum had said no, I had to do it myself. So what's *that* all about, then? There's no point in having a housekeeper if you can't make a mess and expect her to clean it up!

'I think our horses have a *little* more taste than that,' Flo said airily. 'When it comes to biting things, your bottom would be way, way down the list, Lauren Bell.'

'You should come to the stables with us one day, Lauren, and have a go at riding,' Daisy began, for possibly the millionth time since we'd become friends a year ago. 'You never know, you might enjoy it.'

'Thanks, guys, but I think I'll stick to football.' I spotted Dad's Mercedes further along the road and flapped my fingers in farewell at Daisy and Flo. 'See you later. Oh, by the way, I forgot to tell you that the people next door to us have just bought a horse.'

'Really?' Flo looked very interested, and so did Daisy.

'Yes, they're our *neigh*-bours!' I added wickedly, and Flo and Daisy both groaned aloud.

'Lauren, that's the worst joke I ever heard,' Daisy sighed, shaking her head.

Giggling, I scooted off down the road, turning to give Flo and Daisy one last wave. We always had a good laugh together, but there was no way they were getting *me* on a horse!

To my surprise, both Mum *and* Dad were sitting in the car waiting to pick me up. I can't remember the last time that happened. Dad sometimes picks me up on his own, or Gran comes for me. If they can't, I get a lift with Flo or Daisy.

'To what do I owe *this* honour, then?' I asked, climbing in.

'Hey, less of the sarcasm, please, Lolly,' Dad said. I let out a squeal of protest.

'Dad! You haven't called me Lolly since I was about *six*.'

'Yes, well, I wanted to annoy you.' Dad started up the engine. 'Looks like it worked.'

I couldn't help smiling, even though I wanted to be all cool and sulky.

'We just thought we ought to spend some time together as a family before your dad and I go away later this week, Lauren,' Mum explained. 'I left work early.'

'You mean when you abandon me,' I muttered. I couldn't *resist*. I know, I know, I can be a bit of a diva sometimes.

'Let's just enjoy ourselves tonight, shall we,

Lauren?' Mum suggested, a warning note in her voice. 'We thought we'd hit the mall first to buy you some new school shoes, then a quick trip to the hairdresser's to get you a trim and we should *just* have time for a quick snack at Gianni Joe's before we take you to your training session. I've put your sports bag in the boot.'

I nodded. I wanted to play the martyr and be all moody, but I just couldn't keep it up. We always had a fun time when it was just Mum, Dad and me. The downside was, it didn't happen very often... But by the time we got to the mall, we were playing our favourite game, doing impressions of people from the TV, and shrieking with laughter. Dad could do virtually the whole cast of *EastEnders*.

I didn't just get school shoes at the mall. Mum and Dad also bought me a white fake-fur jacket, three T-shirts and a pair of skinny black jeans a bit like Jasmin's, as well as a stash of new make-up. The girl at the counter showed me how to apply it. Then, at the hairdresser's, Mum had booked me a manicure for a surprise, so I came out with glossy, blow-dried hair and pearly pink nails. After stopping off at Gianni Joe's, we headed off to Melfield College for the Stars' first training session of the week. When we arrived, Hannah and Grace were on the front steps waiting for the rest of us, and Jasmin and Georgie were just getting out of Georgie's dad's car. Dad drew to a halt next to them.

'Ooh, look!' Jasmin yelled, pointing at me as I jumped out. 'It's a film star! Can I have your autograph, please?'

I did a twirl, showing off my new jacket, which I'd insisted on wearing.

'Yes, but form an orderly queue,' I said in my best American twang. 'No fighting, no shoving and *definitely* no selling my autograph on eBay!'

Waving at Katy, who'd just hurried through the gates, I lifted the boot of the car to get my footie stuff out. Meanwhile, Jasmin and Georgie peered in over my shoulder at the piles of shopping bags.

'You're just like a celebrity, Lauren,' Jasmin said rather enviously, staring at my beautifully polished nails.

'I swear we're going to see you on the front of *OK!* magazine one of these days,' Georgie remarked, raising her eyebrows. '*Springhill Stars' talented midfielder Lauren Bell relaxes in her palatial home, exhausted after a major shopping spree.*'

Grace, Hannah and Katy had joined us just in time to hear that, and they all grinned, so I forced a smile too. It had just hit me that I didn't really *need* any of this stuff – well, apart from my new school shoes. Were Mum and Dad kind of *bribing* me into behaving myself with Tanya? It was an unpleasant thought, and one I didn't want to examine too closely...

As my mum and dad got out of our car, Freya arrived on her motorbike.

'Hi, girls,' Mum said to the others. 'Lauren, we're just going to let Freya know that Tanya will be bringing you to training on Thursday and to the match on Saturday.'

'Who's Tanya?' Hannah asked curiously, as my parents went across to speak to Freya, who'd taken off her helmet and was shaking out her long blonde hair.

'Our live-in housekeeper,' I explained. 'My mum's got this flash new job, and she's going to be away travelling a lot, like Dad.' I wondered if this could be my opportunity to tell the others exactly how I was feeling, but to my secret dismay, they all burst out laughing.

'Are you *serious*, Lauren?' Katy asked.

I nodded.

'God, Lauren, you're a complete celeb!' Hannah gasped. 'Imagine having a live-in housekeeper – I thought only rich and famous people had those.'

'Oh, wouldn't it be totally fab to have someone else to tidy up after you?' Jasmin said, her eyes wide. 'I'd lie around all day and ask for nachos and dips and Coca-Colas to be brought to me on demand.'

'We have a live-in housekeeper too,' Grace added, her blue eyes dancing. 'She's called Mum.'

Georgie punched me playfully on the shoulder. 'Hey, Lauren, I'm a bit shocked that a posh girl like *you*, with a live-in housekeeper and all, wants to be mates with deadbeats and lowlifes like *us*.'

'Well, you know how it is.' I shrugged, pretending to be just as jokey about it as they were. 'We celebrities have to do our bit for the poor peasants.'

As we cut through the college to get to the changing rooms, the others kept on teasing me, but I gave back as good as I got. You know, I actually *must* be a great actress because none of them seemed to realise how depressed I was about the whole Tanya thing. Not even Grace or Katy, who are really good at spotting that kind of stuff.

'Make way, peasants!' Georgie yelled when we went into the changing-rooms. Ruby, Jo-Jo, Alicia, Debs and Emily, who were all in various stages of undressing, glanced around in surprise. 'I give you Lady Lauren Bell, A-list celebrity and footballing superstar, who now has a live-in housekeeper!'

'Take no notice of her,' I said airily, pushing past Georgie and into the changing-room. 'Just make sure you curtsey before you speak to me.'

Everyone fell about laughing. But as I changed swiftly into my Stars strip, I felt a lump in my throat. I managed to swallow my tears, but when we all ran out onto the pitch, and I saw Mum and Dad on the touchline, I felt even worse.

At our next training session on Thursday evening, my parents wouldn't be there. They'd be hundreds of miles away. And it would be just me and Tanya the Terrible...

On Thursday, there was complete and total silence inside the car as Tanya and I drove towards Melfield College. I'd refused Tanya's offer to sit in the front seat next to her, and I'd climbed sullenly into the back of the Mini. I'd hardly spoken a word to her since she'd picked me up from school a couple of hours earlier and taken me home. Tanya had a meal ready for me, a bowl of chilli and rice, which was *delish*. I had to pretend I didn't like it, although it was a struggle not to scoff it all. Instead I'd filled up on the secret stash of chocolate bars I always kept in my room.

Dad had gone away the day before, to New York, and Mum had left for Italy this morning after dropping me at school. So here I was, alone with Tanya for the next couple of days, and feeling thoroughly miserable and sorry for myself.

'I think you'll be hungry after training, Lauren?' Tanya said as she indicated right to turn into the college car park. 'There's plenty of chilli left. Or I can make you something else?'

I met her eyes in the mirror and looked away. 'Don't bother,' I snapped. 'I'll be fine.'

There was another tense silence. We were a bit early, and none of the other girls had arrived yet. Tanya slid into a parking space and cut the engine. I was about to jump straight out of the car, but she turned to look at me.

'Lauren, I'm sorry that we made a bad start on Monday morning,' she said quietly. 'We don't know each other very well yet, but things will be much better if we can try to get along—'

I rolled my eyes in exasperation. 'Don't you *get* it?' I retorted rudely. 'I don't *want* to get to know you. I don't *want* to get along with you. The only thing I want is for you to leave me alone!'

'Lauren—'

I didn't wait to hear what Tanya had to say. I flung the car door open, grabbed my bag and jumped out. Then I stomped into the college without a backward glance. I was furious and I was upset. I hadn't forgotten Tanya's thoughtless remarks about how 'lucky' I was. Well, at the moment I felt like the unluckiest girl in the whole world...

I was almost changed by the time a bunch of my team-mates arrived, including Jasmin, Hannah and Georgie.

'Hey there, Lauren.' Georgie slapped me on the back as she went over to the lockers. 'We just met your housekeeper standing in the car park, looking a bit lost.'

'Yes, she seems nice.' Hannah sat down and began unlacing her trainers. 'She didn't know where to go, though. Didn't you tell her, Lauren?'

'No,' I replied, trying not to sound guilty. 'I forgot she doesn't know her way around here yet.'

'It's OK, my mum's looking after her,' Jasmin replied, chucking her bag down on the bench.

'Oh, right,' I muttered. 'Well, I'll see you outside, then.'

As I went out of the changing-rooms, I felt a bit annoyed that Hannah and the others seemed to think Tanya was nice. It was all right for them, though. She wasn't living in their house and trying to boss them around. Not that I intended to be bossed around *one bit*...

I collected a football from the big net bag just outside the changing-rooms and took it onto the pitch. Freya was standing on the far touchline, chatting to Tanya and Mrs Sharma, Jasmin's mum. I shot them a glare and then I ignored them and began messing about with the ball, seeing how long I could keep it up in the air without it hitting the ground.

After about five minutes the others came running out, and Freya started us off with some warm-up runs and stretches. Then we played this sort of Follow my Leader game. Everyone stands in line with their own ball, and then the person at the front (Freya picked Georgie) dribbles forward and the rest of us have to copy whatever they do. The front person can do *anything* – like jump up in the air, do a forward roll, run backwards – as long as they keep dribbling the ball.

Georgie was really good at thinking up moves for us to copy, and she led us in a big figure-of-eight shape, doing stepovers and ducking and diving this way and that. She also did a perfect somersault before picking up the ball and going forward again.

The point of the game, Freya had told us, was to practise dribbling a ball while having to keep our heads up to watch the person in front. But after a few minutes, I couldn't resist glancing over at Tanya. I was surprised to see that she was watching me, and to be honest, it irritated me, although I don't know why! She forced a smile, but you can bet your life I did *not* smile back.

Towards the end of the session Freya got us playing a game we really enjoyed. We formed a circle, and Jasmin got chosen to stand in the middle. The people in the circle then had to pass the ball to each other while Jasmin tried to intercept it. The quicker and more accurate the pass, the harder it was for the person in the middle to get hold of the ball. And with Jasmin, you never knew quite what was going to happen anyway. Sometimes she was brilliant, and other times she'd fall and trip over nothing!

This time it took her eight attempts to finally trap the ball.

Then it was my turn to go into the middle, and I got lucky on my very first try. Hannah hit the ball hard to Jo-Jo, but I lunged forward and managed to intercept the pass and get the ball under control with the tip of my boot.

'Excellent, Lauren,' Freya said approvingly.

Someone was applauding me from the sidelines, too. *TANYA!*

'Well done, Lauren,' she called, which completely annoyed me. So I avoided looking at her again for the rest of the training session.

'Well done, the lot of you,' Freya said as, tired and aching, we tramped off the field after the hour was up. 'I reckon we've got a great chance of beating the Swallows on Saturday.'

I glanced over my shoulder and saw Mrs Sharma leading Tanya back to the car park, where they'd wait for us to change and come out. That was when this *really* naughty idea popped into my head. I'd just thought of a way to give Tanya the fright of her life, ha ha...

'Sorry, guys, I have to shoot.' Grace had got changed in double-quick time and was already heading for the door. 'We've got to go and pick Gemma up from her mate's house. See you all Saturday.'

Saturday. My heart sank like a stone inside me. I'd be playing footie on Saturday morning, but after that it would just be me and Tanya at home because Mum and Dad weren't back until Sunday. *Noooooo!*

'Hang on a sec, Grace,' I said quickly, 'what are you all doing on Saturday afternoon? Do you fancy coming round to mine?'

'To Bellingham Palace, you mean?' Georgie said with a huge grin. I couldn't help laughing just a little, although I also made a face at her. 'Sorry, Lauren, I can't. We're going to watch my brother Adey play for Melfield United reserves.'

'I can't, either.' Hannah was concentrating on untying a knot in her bootlaces. 'Mum's taking me shopping.'

Grace was shaking her head too. 'I don't think I can, Lauren. Mum, Gem and me are going to the cinema to see *Angel Face*.'

'Oh, I'm going to see that too!' Jasmin exclaimed. 'My sisters are taking me. It looks good, doesn't it?'

'And we're going to my parents' friends for tea,' Katy said, patting me on the arm. 'Sorry, Lauren.'

I shrugged, pretending not to care, although secretly I'd been hoping that either Grace or Jasmin would invite me to go to the pictures with them.

'Oh, it's no big deal,' I said as Grace waved at us and rushed out. 'I expect I'll pop round to see one of my other mates. My friend Flo has got an indoor swimming pool, and she has the *best* pool parties. Actually my dad's thinking of getting a pool in *our* garden – I bet you'll all want to come round to my house *then*!'

I stopped abruptly, realising that I was sounding a bit boastful and mean. God, *why* did that come out so wrong?

Hannah, Jasmin, Georgie and Katy were staring at me, and they weren't smiling.

'Lauren, we're not mates with you just because your parents are rich, you know,' Georgie said coolly.

'Oh, I know that,' I muttered, feeling my face flame with embarrassment. 'Just take no notice of me, I've had a bad day.'

We got changed pretty much in silence after that, which was *so* unusual for us. Jo-Jo, Ruby and the others kept glancing over at us curiously because we always chatted away non-stop when we were changing. But not tonight.

For my plan to work, I had to be the last to leave. So I got changed very, very slowly. At last I was left alone in the changing rooms, apart from Hannah. And she had her coat on ready to go while I was still packing my muddy kit and boots into my sports bag.

'Don't bother waiting, Hannah.' I took out my make-up bag and went over to the mirror. 'I'll be ages yet.'

'OK,' Hannah replied. 'See you Saturday morning at the game.' She stopped at the door and looked back at me. 'Lauren, are you *sure* you're all right?'

'I'm fine,' I said, smiling brightly. 'See you later.'

Hannah looked as if she was about to say something more, but she didn't. I didn't know whether to feel glad or sorry.

I waited until the sound of Hannah's footsteps had died away down the corridor, then immediately I turned away from the mirror. I grabbed my sports bag, chucked my make-up back in and then tiptoed to the door. Tanya would be waiting for me in the car park, but I wasn't leaving the college by the front entrance. I knew that there was a back way out and a bus stop right outside the back gates where I could get a bus home. I'd done it once before when Dad's car had broken down as he was coming to collect me. Tanya would be totally freaking out when I didn't turn up in the car park...

I took my mobile out of my pocket and turned it off. Then I slipped out of the changing rooms and made my way to the back doors of the college. I hoped I didn't bump into Freya, who was usually the last to leave, because she'd want to know where I was going and then my plan would be ruined. But I met no one.

A few moments later I was out of the doors and walking over to the back gates. I knew Mum and Dad would go completely *mental* if they knew I was on my way home alone. But it wasn't dark yet and the bus stop was right here and hey, *they* were the ones who said it was good for me to be independent – right?

I hurried past the big steel rubbish bins by the gates, and then I got the fright of my life!

'WOOF! WOOF! WOOF!'

The sound of loud barking made me almost jump out of my skin. Petrified, I froze to the spot. I didn't know whether to stay perfectly still or whether to make a run for it. Like I told you before, I'm not very keen on dogs, and, by the noise it was making, this must be a BIG one.

Suddenly a dog trotted out from behind one of the bins. I sagged with relief – it wasn't very big at all. In fact it hardly came up to my knees. It was white and brown – at least, I think it was but it was so filthy, it was hard to tell – and it had quite an ugly face and funny, stumpy little legs.

Panting, the dog bounded over to me, its tongue hanging out, and I began backing away.

'Good dog,' I said anxiously, hoping it didn't lunge at me and take a chunk out of my shin. 'Good boy – or are you a girl?' I didn't like to look!

The dog sat down in front of me and, still panting, cocked its dirty ears. It looked friendly enough, and I could see now that its fat little tail was wagging. That had to be a good sign, didn't it? It seemed to want me to stroke it, but no way was I doing that – I didn't know where it had come from or where it had been!

'OK, doggie, I'm going now,' I said, sidling carefully out of the gates. 'So you be a good boy or girl and go right on home yourself, understand? Bye, then!'

I turned away and hurried off. The bus stop was just a few metres from the gates and I breathed a sigh of relief as I saw on the illuminated information board that the next bus was due in just three minutes.

I glanced down at my watch and gave a little scream of surprise. The dog was sitting at my feet, staring up at me!

'Are you following me?' I asked accusingly. The dog just lifted her leg (I *think* it was a she!) and began scratching herself.

I frowned. The dog looked like a stray and I felt a bit sorry for her, but my bus would be here very soon and there was nothing more I could do.

Or was there?

CHAPTER FOUR

'Lauren? *Lauren!* Are you here?'

I smiled to myself as I stretched out on the sofa in the living room. I could hear the note of panic in Tanya's voice. I'd heard her car pull up on the drive outside, and she'd just rushed into the house, slamming the front door shut behind her.

'Yes,' I called lazily.

I heard Tanya's footsteps running across the hall. A few seconds later she appeared in the living-room doorway. She looked as white as a ghost.

'*Why* didn't you come to meet me in the car park, Lauren?' Tanya demanded furiously. 'You *knew* I was there. I waited for a long time and I was *very* worried and you weren't answering your mobile—'

I shrugged. 'I just thought I'd get the bus home for a change. It's not a crime, is it?'

Tanya looked so angry, I thought she was going to explode. 'You're in my care, Lauren, and if something had happened to you, it would have been *my* fault,' she snapped. 'Please promise me that you will *never* do such a thing again, or I shall have to tell your parents—'

'WOOF! WOOF! WOOF!'

The look on Tanya's face was so comical, I almost burst out laughing.

'What – what's *that*?' she stammered, in complete shock.

'*Well*, this is a bit of a wild guess,' I said, 'but that woof-woof sound probably means there's a dog around somewhere.'

At that very moment, right on cue, the stray dog came trotting in from the hall. I'd left her in the kitchen eating a bowlful of leftover chilli.

Tanya's eyes almost fell out of her head.

'B-but you don't *have* a dog!' she spluttered.

'I do now,' I said gleefully. 'Tanya, meet Chelsea.'

Tail wagging, Chelsea clumped over to Tanya and began sniffing her shoes.

'Please, Lauren,' Tanya said faintly, staring down at Chelsea as if she was seeing things, 'tell me what's going on?'

'Nothing.' I yawned and stood up. 'I found Chelsea outside the college tonight. I think she's a stray, and I'm going to ask my parents if I can keep her.'

'What!' Tanya looked horrified, which secretly delighted me. I knew she'd immediately realised that having a dog around the place would mean a lot of extra work for *her*. Of course, I didn't *really* want a dog, especially an ugly, stinky one like Chelsea. I didn't even *like* dogs. This was all part of my plan.

'I'm going to ring Dad and ask him,' I declared. It had to be Dad and not Mum – I had a much better chance of getting around *him*.

Tanya was still looking shell-shocked, but then she began sniffing the air suspiciously.

'What's that smell?' she asked.

'I can't smell anything,' I said. *I lied!* Chelsea smelt quite bad. In fact, I'd thought it was the college bins that stunk so much, until Chelsea and I got on the bus and no one would sit next to us.

'Is it the dog?' Tanya said, staring down at Chelsea in distaste.

'*You'd* smell bad if you'd been living on the streets, poor little thing,' I said. I bent down and gingerly patted Chelsea's dirty head, making sure I didn't breathe in while I did so. 'I'll ring Dad right now.'

'I want to speak to him too,' Tanya warned me as I went out to the phone on the hall dresser.

'Like, *whatever*,' I muttered. I was pretty pleased with how well my plan had gone so far. Now I just had to make sure Dad played ball.

Chelsea waddled out into the hall with me, and then plumped herself down on my feet when I picked up the phone.

'Not so close, Chelsea,' I said hastily, moving away from her. I wasn't really scared of her any more – she seemed friendly enough. But boy, did she stink! Chelsea seemed to have taken to me, though, and I had no idea why. Couldn't the mutt just *realise* that I'm not a doggie person? I'd brought Chelsea home just to annoy Tanya, and hopefully make her leave. But, hey, I'm not *that* heartless, you know! I'd already decided to make sure that Chelsea went to a good home, eventually.

'Hey, Dad, it's me,' I said as Dad answered his mobile on the third ring. 'Are you OK?'

'Sure, honey,' Dad replied. 'How about you? I don't have long to chat, by the way. I have a meeting in five minutes. But I can call you back later.'

I imagined him sitting in an office at the top of a towering skyscraper, staring out at the Statue of Liberty.

'Oh, this won't take long, Dad,' I said, glancing down the hall. Tanya had gone into the kitchen to take her coat off, but I knew she'd be back. I didn't have much time. 'I found a stray dog tonight after training and I brought her home and I want to keep her. Is that all right?'

'Whoa there, Lauren!' Dad exclaimed. 'Back up a bit. What stray dog is this?'

'I told you, Dad, I found her outside the college tonight.' I put on my best *Daddy's little girl* voice. 'I want to keep her if we can't find her owner. *Please*, Dad.'

There was silence for a moment.

'Have you spoken to your mum about this, Lauren?'

'Not yet,' I said sweetly. 'I wanted to ask you first, Daddy.'

I heard Dad chuckle. 'That figures! Look, poppet, we can't decide this now – my meeting's about to start. Let's wait until your mum and I get home on Sunday, and we can talk about it then.'

'So I can keep the dog till then?' I asked eagerly. I'd been banking on Dad giving in easily because he felt guilty about leaving me with Tanya – and it looked like it had worked!

'Fine,' Dad replied. 'As long as Tanya's happy about it.'

'She's cool, Dad.' I heard Tanya hurrying out of the kitchen. 'Thanks, see you Sunday.'

Just then Tanya appeared in the hallway. She looked extremely annoyed when she saw that I'd already hung up.

'Sorry, Dad didn't have time to speak to you,' I said coolly. 'He was just about to go into a meeting.'

Tanya frowned. 'And what did he say about the dog?' she demanded.

'Oh, that's all fine,' I announced, trying not to sound *too* smug. Maybe Tanya would have had enough by Sunday and resign as soon as my parents came home. Well, I could hope! 'Chelsea can stay – for the moment, anyway. And I *bet* Dad will let me keep her.' I stared challengingly at Tanya. 'He lets me have almost everything I want.'

Tanya looked even more annoyed. But before either of us could say anything, we heard a key in the lock and the front door swung open.

'Hello, darling. Hello, Tanya.' Gran came in, wrapped up snugly in a black wool coat and fur-topped boots. 'Goodness me, it's cold out there, isn't it? Very bad for my arthritis. My doctor says—'

Suddenly Gran caught sight of Chelsea, who'd climbed off my feet and was shuffling towards her, tongue lolling. Gran looked so shocked I was ready to leap forward and catch her because I thought she was going to faint!

'What – what's *that*?' Gran shrieked rather melodramatically.

'A dog,' Tanya and I replied together.

Gran seemed rooted to the spot as Chelsea began sniffing her boots. Then Chelsea gave a little growl, lunged forward and began tugging at the fur around the top.

'Help!' Gran tried to pull away, but Chelsea hung on for grim death. 'It's attacking me!'

'I'll save you, Gran!' I yelled, trying not to laugh. But it *was* funny! Grabbing Chelsea, I pulled her off.

'Now, will somebody *please* tell me what's going on?' Gran gasped, edging warily around Chelsea towards the living room. 'Where has this – this *dog* come from?'

'I think she's a stray,' I replied. 'I found her outside Melfield College tonight.'

Gran was already reaching for the phone. 'Well, the best thing to do is to ring the RSPCA and they'll come and collect her.'

'*No*, Gran.' I kept a tight hold of Chelsea, trying not to shudder with horror as she licked my hand with her wet, sloppy tongue. 'I rang Dad, and he said I can keep her for the moment.'

'Oh, Lauren, don't be ridiculous!' Gran looked aghast. 'Just look at the state of the poor little thing. You don't know where it's been! It might have all sorts of diseases. The RSPCA will look after it and find it a good home—' She paused, sniffing the air. 'What *is* that smell?'

'I'm not sure,' I said airily. 'Chelsea and I will be in my room if anyone wants us.'

And leaving Gran with Tanya, I shot up the stairs with Chelsea at my heels, barking loudly. God, why were dogs so *noisy*! Anyway, there was *nothing* Gran or Tanya could do about the dog, now that

I'd got Dad's permission. Secretly I congratulated myself on speaking to Dad first before Tanya and Gran got in there. *Yay, me!*

My bedroom was on the second floor of the house, and I also had my own en-suite bathroom. When Hannah, Katy and the others had come round to ours for the first time, just after Mum and I had got back from Florida, I'd shown them my room, and Georgie had said that it must be like sleeping in Wembley Stadium every night. That was a bit over the top though – it's not *that* big!

I opened a window when Chelsea and I went in, but it was still a bit whiffy. So I grabbed a bottle of Chanel perfume my parents had given me for Christmas and sprayed it around a bit. Chelsea went mad at the noise of the spray and began snapping her teeth, trying to catch the mist of perfume as it wafted around the room.

'So you've got expensive tastes, huh, Chelsea?' I said with a grin. The dog really *could* do with a bath, but I wasn't very confident about washing her on my own, and I was absolutely sure that neither Tanya nor Gran would help me. Gran would probably have a heart attack at the very thought!

My bedroom had just been redecorated in cream

and purple, and I was a bit worried about Chelsea messing it up. But I found an old blanket in the linen chest on the landing, and Chelsea seemed perfectly happy to lie on the blanket next to the computer desk while I spent a couple of hours online, chatting to Flo, Daisy and other mates from school. But she did start barking every time she heard footsteps on the stairs outside my door, which drove me *nuts*.

Gran came up a couple of times to talk to me. She'd rung my dad and tried to persuade him to let her call the RSPCA to take Chelsea away, but Dad had explained that I wanted to keep the dog for the moment and try to find her owner. *Go, Dad!* Apparently Tanya was also in a mood because Chelsea had upset the bowl and there were chilli stains all over the clean kitchen floor. So everything was going just fine!

By the time I went to bed, I was hardly noticing the smell any more, either, which was a bonus. Maybe I was just getting used to it, I thought sleepily, as I drifted off. Chelsea was on her blanket, curled up on the floor near the bed, and I could hear her snuffling and wheezing a little. It had taken *ages* to get her settled because she kept trying to climb up on to the bed with me, but no way was I having that!

I drifted off to sleep, feeling very pleased with the way things were going. But in the middle of the night, Chelsea woke up and started whining and scratching one of the bedposts.

'Chelsea! Stop that!' I muttered, dazed and barely half-awake. *God, why would anyone want a dog?* I thought drowsily as I slipped back into sleep again. They were a complete pain in the butt with their barking and whining and their constant demands. And as for that doggy smell...

Even worse, when I woke up again next morning, there was a *different* kind of doggy smell in the room. I sat up, pushing my hair off my face, and saw a pile of poo right in the middle of the purple and white bedside rug. EEK!

'Chelsea!' I groaned, staggering out of bed and being *extremely* careful where I put my feet.

Chelsea sat up on her blanket, looking a bit crestfallen as if she knew she'd done something wrong. It wasn't her fault, I knew, as I ran downstairs to get some clean-up stuff. It just hadn't occurred to me that she might need to *go* in the night.

I was glad that it was early and Tanya wasn't up

yet. But I was certainly beginning to realise that keeping Chelsea, even for a short time, wasn't going to be as simple as I'd thought...

'So, is that your new housekeeper, then, Lauren?' Daisy asked curiously as we wandered towards the school gates at the end of Friday afternoon.

'Yes,' I replied through gritted teeth. Tanya was standing at the gates, waving at me like I was some kind of five-year-old kid. I was *sooo* embarrassed in front of Flo and Daisy.

'She looks OK,' Daisy whispered.

'She isn't,' I said. 'She feeds me on bread and water and locks me in the cellar. What are you two doing tomorrow, by the way?'

'We're competing in a gymkhana.' Flo raised her eyebrows at me. 'Want to come and watch?'

'No, sorry, I'm busy,' I lied quickly. A gymkhana with lots of scary horses around sounded like my idea of hell. So it looked like it was just going to be me and Chelsea holed up in my room tomorrow after the game against the Swallows, while everyone else was out having fun...

I hadn't mentioned Chelsea to Flo or Daisy. It was partly because I knew I wouldn't be keeping her, so there was no point in telling them. But – and this does sound *mean* – it was also because I was a bit ashamed of her. Flo had a white pedigree Persian cat, and Daisy had got a spaniel puppy for her birthday last month. My friends' pets were *supermodels* next to ugly little Chelsea. If only I could give her a bath, I mused, as we reached the gates. She might look a bit better then...

'Hello, Lauren,' Tanya said as we reached the gates.

I ignored her, then wished I hadn't as I saw that Flo and Daisy looked rather shocked. 'See you Monday,' I said to them. They nodded and went over to their parents' cars. They kept looking back at me and Tanya, and I just *knew* they were talking about us.

'Are those your friends?' Tanya asked, leading the way to her car which was parked a little way along the road.

'Yes, and I don't like being embarrassed in front of them,' I retorted. 'Why didn't you just sit in the car and wait for me? That's what Mum and Dad do.'

'Because I wanted to be sure you didn't decide to take the *bus* home again,' Tanya said calmly.

I glared at her as we climbed into the Mini. This time I couldn't get into the back seat because it was covered with bulging bags from the supermarket.

'How's Chelsea?' I asked abruptly. 'Did you buy some dog food for her?'

'Yes.' Looking rather harassed, Tanya started the car. 'I shut her safely in the kitchen before I went shopping.'

I smiled to myself. The mere *mention* of Chelsea seemed to stress Tanya out. I'd noticed dog hairs all over the living room, the stairs and my bedroom, and I wondered if Tanya had had to vacuum the house again today. I knew she'd already cleaned the place yesterday morning.

We drove home in silence. When we got there, I automatically started helping Tanya to get the shopping bags off the back seat and out of the boot without thinking about it. I was a bit annoyed with myself, but, you know, I'm not *such* a bad person, am I? I didn't have anything against Tanya, really, I suppose. Apart from the fact that she'd said I was spoilt. It was mostly the situation I didn't like. But I was still determined to get rid of her...

'Oh, Gran's here,' I said as we carried the

shopping bags through the front door into the hall. Gran's jacket was hanging on the coat-stand.

'Lauren? Tanya?' Gran called in a trembling voice from the kitchen. 'Is that you?'

'Nope, Gran, we're burglars,' I called naughtily.

We took the bags straight through to the kitchen. Well, Chelsea might have been safe in there, but the kitchen wasn't safe from Chelsea...

What a sight met our eyes. Gran was standing with her back pressed against one of the black granite worktops, looking as if she was about to faint. The doors of one of the glossy cream cupboards under the double sink were open, and the tiled floor was *covered* – and I mean covered – in hundreds of tiny shreds of white paper. Meanwhile Chelsea was stretched out under the big glass table in the corner, chewing on a roll of cardboard.

'What's happened?' Tanya cried.

I couldn't help grinning. I'd already worked it out in a flash. 'It's kitchen paper,' I said, bending to look at the floor more closely as Chelsea bounded out to say hello. 'Gran, what *have* you been up to?'

'Lauren, this is no time for silly jokes!' Gran said crossly. 'That *dog* has obviously managed to open up the cupboard, pull out a roll of kitchen paper and tear it to bits!'

Suddenly Tanya gave a cry of dismay and leapt forward. 'My shoes!'

There in the corner by the huge American-style fridge-freezer were the flat black shoes that Tanya wore when she was cleaning the house. Well, she wouldn't be wearing *those* again. The shoes had been chewed completely out of shape.

'Oh, Chelsea,' I patted her grubby head, trying hard not to burst out laughing. 'You *are* a naughty girl!'

I could tell Tanya was absolutely furious as she held the shoes out at arm's length. Meanwhile Gran looked like she was going to need smelling salts to revive her.

'Lauren, that dog smells so bad, it's making me feel ill!' she declared. 'You simply *have* to give her a bath.'

'OK, Gran, but I'll need some help.' I'd just had an idea. 'I'll get a few mates round. Come on, Chelsea.'

'There'll be no dinner for a while, Lauren,' Tanya called out to me in a clipped voice. 'I have to clean up this mess first.'

'No problem,' I replied breezily. 'I would help, but, like Gran says, Chelsea needs a bath!'

Then I grabbed my phone from my school bag and sent the same text to Grace, Georgie, Hannah, Katy and Jasmin.

What u up 2? Pamper party and munchies at mine 2nite! Hope u can make it x

The doorbell pealed out about half an hour or so later, and I rushed to answer it. Jasmin, Katy and Georgie were standing on the doorstep, and just behind them I could see Hannah and Grace climbing out of Mr Fleetwood's car.

'Great to see you guys,' I said, ushering them all in. 'This is going to be a pamper party you'll never forget, believe me.'

'Do we get to play with all that new make-up your parents bought you on Tuesday?' Grace asked eagerly.

'Actually, no,' I said, opening the living-room door. 'The pamper party isn't for *us*—'

I didn't get a chance to say anything more. Chelsea came barrelling out of the living room like a super-charged rocket and hurled herself at the nearest person, which happened to be Jasmin.

'Help!' Jasmin leapt backwards in fright as Chelsea jumped up at her knees. 'Lauren, what's going on?'

'Girls, meet my dog, Chelsea,' I announced. I couldn't help laughing at Jasmin's round-eyed look of shock.

Realising that Jasmin was a bit of a lost cause, Chelsea turned to Grace and began snuffling around her red ballet flats.

'Hello, girl.' Grace got down on her knees and tickled Chelsea behind her ears. 'You're a funny-looking little thing, aren't you?' Then she sniffed and frowned. 'Oh God, Lauren, I think I can guess who this pamper party's for!'

'Where did you get her, Lauren?' Georgie asked, stroking Chelsea's back. 'I've got to say, she's not *exactly* the kind of pet I'd expect to see at Bellingham Palace!'

'I found her outside the college on Tuesday,' I replied.

'And you're keeping her?' Hannah asked, surprised.

I nodded. 'For the moment, anyway.' I didn't want to go into *too* many details. 'But she needs a bath, as you can tell.' Katy and Jasmin were holding their noses by now. 'Will you give me a hand?'

'No problem,' Grace agreed. 'Have you checked her for fleas, by the way?'

'FLEAS!' I shrieked, immediately feeling itchy all over. 'No, I haven't.'

Grace pulled her phone out of her pocket. 'Look, I'll ring Mum and ask her to drop Lewis's flea shampoo round – I'm sure she won't mind, she's got to go out soon to take Gemma to her ballet class, anyway. In the meantime, we can run the bath.'

Secretly I was really glad that Grace was taking charge. She knew loads about dogs, and I didn't know *anything*. Why would I, though? I *hate* dogs!

At that moment Tanya appeared in the doorway. Gran had tottered home for a lie-down about ten minutes ago, after helping Tanya to clear up the kitchen.

'Hello again, girls,' Tanya said warmly. Then she looked right at me, and her gaze was challenging. 'Lauren, shall I make some drinks and snacks for you and your friends? You can have them after you've bathed the dog.'

'OK,' I muttered uncomfortably. I could feel the others staring at me and forced myself to add, 'Thanks.'

There was silence as Tanya nodded and went off.

'Have you and Tanya had a row, Lauren?' Katy asked quietly.

I was *totally* embarrassed by now. 'Not really,' I mumbled. 'Shall we go and run the bath?'

We all went upstairs to the main bathroom on the first floor, Chelsea galumphing happily along behind us.

'God, Lauren, I hope we don't make too much mess,' Hannah said, gazing round at the dazzlingly shiny white and silver tiles, the enormous roll-top bath and the fluffy white towels.

'Oh, don't worry, Tanya'll clean it up,' I said dismissively. Then I felt bad again as the girls glanced knowingly at each other. 'Well, she *is* the housekeeper, isn't she?' I reminded them as Georgie turned on the taps.

By the time Mrs Kennedy arrived with the shampoo, the bath was half-full, we'd shrouded the room with old towels to mop up any mess and Chelsea was good to go. Grace had put a smear of Vaseline around Chelsea's eyes and two bits of cotton wool in her droopy little ears.

'To stop the water getting in,' she explained. 'Where's Chelsea's lead, Lauren? We can put that on, just to keep her under control a bit.'

'She doesn't have one,' I replied.

Grace looked amazed. 'Well, how do you take her for walks, then?'

You know what? I hadn't even *thought* about taking Chelsea for a walk. How stupid am I? Maybe that's why she'd attacked the kitchen roll, because she was bored and had too much energy…

'I'll buy one tomorrow,' I murmured, feeling like the worst person in the *world*. OK, so I didn't like dogs, but I'd brought Chelsea home and so I ought to be looking after her a little better. 'Let's do this, guys, shall we?'

We all gathered around Chelsea, got a firm hold of her and lifted her into the bath. She whined and struggled a bit, but she calmed down when I spoke gently to her.

'Look, she's *actually* white under all that dirt!' Jasmin said, as she sponged Chelsea's back.

'Who's a good girl, then?' Hannah cooed, scratching Chelsea's ear. 'We had a dog up until last year, then Sam got ill and had to be put to sleep. I really miss him. I think I'll ask my parents if I can get a puppy.'

'I love our Lewis to absolute bits,' Grace confided, up to her arms in soapy water. 'He's like one of the family. Anyone else got any pets?'

'We had a dog when we lived in Poland.' Katy looked a bit sad. 'We couldn't bring him with us, so now he lives with my grandmother and grandfather.'

'We've got a cat called Rainbow,' Georgie joined in.

'And I've got a chinchilla,' added Jasmin, very unexpectedly. 'Her name's Ludmilla.'

'Ludmilla the chinchilla?' Georgie said, raising her eyebrows, and we all burst into loud giggles.

'Don't laugh!' Jasmin said indignantly. 'She's cuddly and gorgeous and I *love* her!'

'Typical Jasmin not to have an ordinary pet like a dog or a cat,' Georgie said, still giggling.

Jasmin grinned. 'I like to be different,' she said.

'Really?' Grace glanced at Jasmin's bright pink tights, teamed with black patent flats, a flippy, spotty pink and white skirt and a red hoodie. 'I'd never have guessed!'

I was silent as the others chattered on about their pets. They seemed to be ever so fond of them. That made me feel bad because, to be perfectly honest with you, I was beginning to feel slightly guilty about bringing Chelsea home with me just to annoy Tanya. I knew that I was using the dog to get my own way. But, honestly, even though I didn't want to keep Chelsea myself, I really *was* determined to make sure that she was looked after. That might mean tracing her original owner, or it might mean finding her a new home. The little dog would be a winner whatever happened, I consoled myself.

'So, what's the story with you and Tanya, then, Lauren?' Georgie asked, completely out of the blue, as we lifted Chelsea carefully out of the bath and placed her on the floor. She was as clean as a whistle now, but sadly, she still looked pretty ugly!

'Quick, get that towel around Chelsea before she shakes herself,' Grace instructed. 'EEEK – too late!'

We all shrieked with laughter as Chelsea shook herself furiously and drops of soapy water went everywhere, including all over us. Secretly, though, I was glad I didn't have to answer Georgie's question.

'Well, at least you're clean now, Chelsea,' Katy remarked, towelling the dog dry. 'But I still don't think you're going to win any beauty contests!'

'OK, Lauren, now don't hold out on us.' Georgie was staring at me again with that annoyingly direct gaze of hers. 'You and Tanya, what's going on?'

I might have known Georgie wouldn't give up

that easily. Katy, Jasmin, Hannah and Grace were looking very curious too.

'There's *nothing* going on,' I said as coolly as I could. 'OK, so I wasn't too happy when Mum and Dad hired her. But I'm a big girl now. I can stand it.'

'And how does Tanya feel about Chelsea?' asked Hannah.

'Yes, she's only been here a few days, and suddenly you've got a dog?' Grace added. 'That must be a lot of extra work for her.'

I flushed red hot with embarrassment and had to bend over to pet Chelsea to hide my face.

'Tanya's OK with it,' I muttered. 'Anyway, it's not up to her, it's down to Mum and Dad. Let's go and have some munchies now, shall we?'

I might have known the girls would guess something was going on, I reflected ruefully later that evening. The others had gone a few hours ago, and I was lying on my bed, watching TV, with Chelsea curled up on the purple velvet throw beside me. Now that she was clean, I'd decided to let her sleep on the bed, just so I could get a bit of peace without her whining and trying to jump up next to me.

I sighed. Even though I'd only been mates with

Jasmin, Grace, Hannah, Georgie and Katy for a couple of months or so and we still didn't know each other *that* well, it hadn't taken long for them to suss out that Tanya and I had 'issues'. I longed to confide in them, but, because I was the youngest of the group, I was just so worried that they'd think I was childish and silly for wanting more of my mum and dad's time, especially when their hard work provided this fabulous lifestyle for us. The others seemed to think I had *everything* a girl could ever want...

Chelsea was resting her head on my legs and she started twitching and snuffling a little in her sleep. I sighed again, louder this time. Tomorrow I'd have to get up early and go to the pet shop to buy a lead. *Then* I'd have to take Chelsea for a walk before the match.

God, all this feeding and walking and bathing and clearing up messes seemed like a lot of hard work. The cuddles were quite nice, I suppose, and the weight of Chelsea's soft warm body against my legs made me feel less lonely, but I'm not a doggie person at all. Honestly, I'm just *not*.

CHAPTER FIVE

'Lauren, we *can't* take Chelsea to the match!' Tanya said furiously for about the tenth time. 'I'm sure your coach – what's her name, Freya? – would not like it.'

I shrugged. We were standing on the drive by Tanya's car, and I had my sports bag in one hand and Chelsea's new lead in the other. Chelsea, meanwhile, was sitting patiently at my feet, scratching herself vigorously ever so often.

'Freya won't care,' I retorted, sneaking a quick glance at my watch. We were already late. I'd got up really early to buy a dog collar and lead, and then

I'd taken Chelsea to the park for a walk. *Nightmare!* I'd let Chelsea off the lead and then she wouldn't come back when I called her. I'd ended up chasing her round the park and finally capturing her by the gates when she was just about to run out on to the busy road. I was exhausted and hot and flustered by the time we got home, ten minutes after we should already have left for the match.

'But, Lauren—'

'Look, we *could* leave her here, but who knows what damage she might cause while we're away?' I pointed out. 'It's your call.'

Tanya hesitated for a moment, then she sighed.

'All right, Lauren, You win this time. There's a blanket in the boot. Put that on the back seat for her.'

Smiling triumphantly, I did as Tanya said. Chelsea's legs were too small and stumpy to jump into the car so I had to lift her in. Then I sat down beside her in the back.

'She won't – you know – *do* anything, will she?' Tanya asked nervously as we set off. 'I mean *toilet* things.'

'I don't know,' I replied, trying not to laugh. 'She might.'

That made Tanya put her foot down and speed up a little! Secretly, I didn't think Chelsea would want to 'go' as she'd already 'been' at the park that morning. I even had to clear it up, would you believe? A little old lady walking a Yorkshire terrier had given me a plastic bag from the stash in her pocket, and then shown me the special bin to put it in. YUK! Owning a dog is like living in a whole different, weird world, isn't it?

When we reached the college, I glanced at my watch again. It was only five minutes to kick-off.

'OK, no misbehaving on the touchline, Chelsea,' I said, tickling the dog's dumpy little tummy. 'And make sure you cheer loudly for the Stars!'

I handed Chelsea's lead to Tanya and jumped out of the Mini. Chelsea whined and began trying to follow me, but I closed the door quickly.

'Lauren!' Tanya wound the window down, looking outraged. 'I thought we were going to leave her in the car?'

I was shaking my head. 'Sorry, Tanya, can't do that. It's against the law in England to leave an animal locked up in a car. Haven't you seen those RSPCA posters? See you later.'

And I bounced off gleefully, leaving Tanya to look

after Chelsea. I didn't actually know if it *was* against the law, but I was betting that Tanya, being foreign, didn't know either!

The changing-rooms were empty when I dashed in. I stripped off and got into my kit in record time and then ran out onto the pitch. The Stars and the Swallows were just getting into position, ready for kick-off.

'Sorry, Freya,' I gasped as I raced past her.

'Lauren, you're here!' Freya looked very annoyed, but relieved too. 'I thought we might have to cancel.'

'Sorry!' I said again. The Stars occasionally had a sub or two available, but sometimes it was a struggle to put out a full team if someone was sick or away on holiday. I already knew that Emily Barnard had flu, as she wasn't at training on Thursday, and I could see Hattie Richards, one of our occasional subs, had already taken Emily's place for today.

I whizzed over to my place just as Grace placed the ball in the centre circle.

'Nice of you to join us, Lady Lauren,' Jasmin called with a wink.

'WOOF! WOOF! WOOF!'

All the players on the pitch, and the ref too, turned to look at Chelsea. She was standing on the touchline with Tanya, barking her head off. Her big sad brown eyes were fixed on me, and she was straining at the lead to get away from Tanya, who looked extremely embarrassed.

The game began. Then it was *my* turn to start feeling embarrassed. I was straight into the action after about ten seconds when Hannah slid the ball smoothly towards me.

'WOOF! WOOF!'

I almost jumped out of my skin as Chelsea started barking again. For a moment I hesitated, and that hesitation was fatal. One of the Swallows defenders swooped down on me and robbed me of the ball. Gritting my teeth with annoyance, I chased after her. Jasmin was already on to it as well, and between us we managed to hassle the Swallows' girl off the ball. Jasmin passed it quickly to me, and I set off on one of my trademark runs down the wing.

'WOOF! WOOF! WOOF!' followed me all the way to the Swallows' penalty area, until I side-footed the ball to Hannah. She took a shot, but it bobbled past the post.

'Chelsea's cheering you on, then!' Jasmin said

with a wink, as we waited for the goal kick.

'Putting me off, more like!' I muttered.

Chelsea barked furiously every single time I touched the ball, but after a while I started to get used to it. Then, when Keira Cumberland, one of the Swallows' players, tackled me and accidentally knocked me over, Chelsea went *mad*. She leapt up and down and barked and whined and bared her teeth. Then she started growling at Keira every time she went over to that side of the field. Keira burst into tears because apparently she *hates* dogs. Oh, it was all fun and games! Grace scored two goals in the first half and Fiona Benson got one back for the Swallows, but that was *nothing* compared to all the excitement that Chelsea caused.

'Chelsea's the star of the show, Lauren,' Georgie laughed as we went off at half-time.

'She sure is,' I replied with a wink. 'Maybe we should put her in the team?'

'I know it's funny, Lauren,' Grace said as we all piled into the changing-rooms, 'but you ought to think about getting some training for Chelsea. She'd be much easier to control then. I can give you the name and phone number of the dog trainer we took Lewis to, if you like.'

'All right,' I agreed, although I wasn't really interested. Chelsea's next owner might be, though, so I might as well have the trainer's name to pass on.

'Just to warn you, Lauren,' Katy whispered in my ear as Freya strode into the changing-rooms, 'I don't think Freya was too impressed!'

But Freya didn't say anything about Chelsea. Well, not till the end of her half-time talk, anyway. As we were going back out onto the pitch, she beckoned me to stay behind.

'Lauren, I've asked Tanya if she'll walk your dog around the college grounds while we're playing the second half,' she said briskly. 'She's distracting you, as well as the rest of the players, and she's getting on everyone's nerves.'

'Oh, Tanya's not *that* bad,' I said with a grin.

'Not funny, Lauren,' Freya replied coolly.

'Sorry.' Secretly, I was delighted. Tanya would be bored stiff!

'And, Lauren.' Freya's direct blue eyes stared piercingly into my own. 'I don't know what's going on with you and Tanya, but Chelsea is most definitely banned from next week's game with the Blackbridge Belles. You know exactly how much both teams always want to win these derby matches, and I don't want *any* distractions. Is that clear?'

'Yes, Freya,' I muttered. The Blackbridge Belles were our biggest rivals and even though there was nothing at stake for either club this season as we were both out of the running for promotion, competition would be fierce.

Still, by this time next week, I might not even have Chelsea any more. It all depended on my parents. And who knows? Tanya might not be here by this time next week either, if my plan worked...

'Lauren? I'm home!'

'Hiya, Mum.'

Dad and I were in his study. He was reading the Sunday newspapers, and I was checking my emails on his computer. Dad had got home from New York earlier that morning and taken me out for lunch, just me and him. We'd had a great laugh, and I'd told him all about yesterday's match against the Swallows, which we'd eventually won 3–1. I'd even got a goal in the second half myself – and, even better, Tanya obviously hadn't enjoyed walking aimlessly around with Chelsea while we played the rest of the game, ha ha!

Now it was late afternoon, and Mum was back

too. I jumped up from the desk and went out into the hall, Dad following behind me.

Mum had put her suitcase down and was taking off her black jacket. Her face broke into a smile when she saw me. Dropping her jacket carelessly on top of the suitcase, she hurried over and gave me a huge hug.

'I missed you, sweetie,' she murmured into my hair. 'How are you? How are you getting on with Tanya?'

Luckily she didn't wait for a reply before turning to give my dad a kiss on the cheek. 'Are you OK, Nathan? How was your flight?'

'Dull and boring, but on time at least,' Dad replied, kissing her back. He put his arms around both me and Mum and gave us a squeeze. 'It's good to be together again, isn't it?'

Mum nodded. 'Yes, and I hate to break this up,' she said with a frown, 'but there appears to be something sniffing around my ankles.'

I giggled as I broke away from the circle of Dad's arms. 'Chelsea's feeling left out,' I declared. 'Say hello to Chelsea, Mum.'

Chelsea stopped investigating Mum's elegant black stiletto-heeled court shoes, and sat back on her chubby haunches. She stared up at Mum, cocking her funny, ugly face to one side.

'*This* is Chelsea?' Mum queried faintly.

Dad nodded. 'That's what I said,' he remarked drily. 'Odd-looking little thing, isn't she?'

I gave him a shove. '*Dad!* She'll hear you. She's very intelligent, you know.' I know, I know, but I had to pretend I really loved her. It was all part of my plan, remember?

Mum bent down and cautiously patted Chelsea's head. Chelsea immediately rolled over, an ecstatic look on her face, showing her podgy tum.

'Isn't she cute?' I said, trying to sound like I really meant it. But Mum and Dad didn't look very convinced.

'Are you *sure* you want to keep her, Lauren?' Mum asked doubtfully as she and I went into the living room, Chelsea waddling along behind us. Dad had popped to the kitchen to ask Tanya to make us some tea. 'You know, I don't think it's a bad idea for you to have a pet, as long as you're responsible for looking after it. But your dad and I would be happy to buy you a pedigree puppy or kitten, like your friends have.'

I was silent. I knew what Mum was getting at. She

and Dad thought I should have a beautiful pedigree pet to go with their image and their lifestyle, and Chelsea just didn't *fit*. Suddenly I wondered what would have happened if *I* hadn't turned out to be the kind of daughter that Mum and Dad were expecting. I was blonde and I was slim and people had always said that I was pretty, and I knew Mum and Dad loved me, even if they *were* always working. But would they have loved me so much if I *hadn't* been all of those things?

Unexpectedly, a big, teary lump rose in my throat and almost choked me. I had to swallow several times before I could speak. Chelsea was jumping up at my legs, and annoying me. Irritably I pushed her away. Chelsea looked very downcast and began whining, so I lifted her onto my lap just to shut her up.

'I'd like to keep her, Mum, but I think we should look for her owner first,' I said carefully. 'Someone might be desperate to find her.'

This was the plan I'd worked out over the last few days. It could take *ages* to find Chelsea's original owner, giving me plenty of time to continue annoying Tanya. She hadn't said anything to me about Chelsea's behaviour on Saturday at the match, but I could see that she was embarrassed and annoyed about it. She was even *more* annoyed when Chelsea left a whole load of dog hairs in the back of her car, *tee hee*.

'That sounds like a good idea, darling,' Mum said, trying not to look too relieved as Dad came in. 'Nat, Lauren's suggested that we don't make any decisions about Chelsea yet. We're going to look for her owner first.'

Dad nodded. He grinned at Chelsea, who was now lying contentedly in my arms, a bit like a baby.

'She's a soppy one, isn't she? OK, that's what we'll do, then. We can start by contacting the RSPCA and any other local animal charities.' He glanced at Mum. 'We'd better run this by Tanya, though, Alyssa.'

THIS IS IT, I thought, my heart beginning to thump with anticipation. *By this evening, Tanya might be gone – hooray!* I'd already decided to *beg* Mum and Dad not to replace her. I was convinced that we could manage when they were away if we roped in as many people as we could find to look after me – Gran, Mrs Melvyn, my uncles and aunts and even my mates' parents, hopefully.

'When are you going away again, Dad?' I asked.

'Next Friday, just for a couple of nights,' he replied, casually tickling Chelsea under her chin. 'But I think your mum's at home all next week, now.'

'Great!' I exclaimed. Even better. There was no need for Tanya to be here if Mum was going to be at home. She could leave right now if she wanted to! 'Will you come to the derby game against the Blackbridge Belles next Saturday, Mum?'

Mum nodded, and I beamed at her as Tanya appeared with the tea tray.

'I'll leave you to *talk*, then,' I said innocently. I put Chelsea down on the floor and stood up. 'I'm going up to my room.'

'Welcome back, Mrs Bell,' Tanya said with a smile, handing out the teacups as I left. Chelsea came with me, stuck to my heels like superglue, as usual.

'Thank you, Tanya,' I heard Mum say. Carefully, I left the living-room door ajar before I went over to the stairs. I got about halfway up, making a lot of noise about it, and stopped. Then I tiptoed down quietly again. Chelsea sat on the bottom step, staring at me with her head on one side as if she thought I was mad.

'…and you see, the dog makes a lot of extra work for me, Mrs Bell,' Tanya was saying firmly. 'I like animals, but it is very difficult.'

I smiled to myself.

'I'm sure we could increase your wages a little to cover the extra work you're doing if you'll stay, Tanya,' my mum said. 'You're doing a good job, and we don't want to lose you.'

'And, as you know, Tanya, we decided on a three-month probation period,' Dad added. My ears pricked up. No one had told me about this! 'The deal, if you remember, was that you could leave within that period if you wished, or we could ask you to leave if things didn't work out. Either way, we'd pay you for the full three months. Now, what would you like to do?'

There was silence, and I held my breath.

'I will stay,' Tanya said at last, and I pulled a face at the living-room door. Still, I wasn't about to give up yet! Tanya had sounded quite depressed, which gave me hope. I turned away and was about to tiptoe upstairs when I saw the shape of someone standing in the front porch, about to ring the bell. I sprang forward and opened the door.

'Oh, hello, darling.' Gran came in. It was a mild

day, but as usual, she was dressed for a trip to the North Pole. 'Is your mum back? I just thought I'd pop round and say hello.'

'Yes, she's in the living room. She and Dad are talking to Tanya. How are you, Gran?'

Gran heaved a sigh. 'Well, I mustn't grumble. But I've had these rather strange pains in my hands for the last few days. My doctor said—' She stopped as she saw Chelsea lying on the bottom stair, wagging her tail. 'The dog's still here, then?'

'Yep, unless you're hallucinating, Gran,' I replied with a grin. 'Maybe you'd better go and see your doctor!' I patted Chelsea's head and she licked my hand. 'No, you're not seeing things, she's definitely real.'

'In that case...' Gran opened her cream and gilt designer handbag and took out, of all things, a blue rubber bone. I stared at it in disbelief.

'Someone donated it to the shop,' Gran explained. I don't think I told you that Gran works as a volunteer in one of the charity shops in the high street. She's got a good heart. 'It's second-hand, but there are a few too many teeth marks to sell it. I thought Chelsea might like it.'

'Thanks, Gran.' I took the bone and held it out to

Chelsea. She immediately grasped it in her teeth and began gnawing at it, making funny little growling sounds in the back of her throat.

'So what did your mum and dad say about the dog?' Gran asked, removing her cream cashmere coat.

'We're going to look for Chelsea's owner before we make any decisions,' I explained. 'She's staying here in the meantime.'

Gran raised her eyebrows at me. 'And what does Tanya think about *that*?'

'I don't know,' I said with a shrug.

And I hadn't told Mum, Dad or Gran this yet, but even if we found Chelsea's owner, I wasn't going to hand her over to just *anybody*. If I didn't think they were going to treat Chelsea properly, they wouldn't be getting her back. Simple as that.

CHAPTER SIX

You know what? This is *really* weird, but I'm almost beginning to enjoy taking Chelsea for walks twice a day. It's not so great if it's cold or wet, of course, but Chelsea doesn't seem to care.

It poured with rain yesterday and she loved splashing through all the puddles. I decided that next time I'd put my pink and purple polka-dot wellies on and join her! I don't think Tanya was too impressed with Chelsea's muddy paw prints all over the kitchen floor though... It was Wednesday now, three days after I'd listened in on her conversation with Mum and Dad, and I still had high hopes that she'd be gone by the end of the week.

Tonight I'd had the brilliant idea of texting the others and asking them to meet Chelsea and me in the park while we were having our walk, if they weren't doing anything and didn't have too much homework. OK, I know I saw them yesterday at training and I'd see them again tomorrow, but there's always more stuff to gossip about, isn't there? Katy had replied, apologising that she couldn't come, but the others were up for it.

As I led Chelsea down the path towards the football field where we always hung out, I saw that Grace, Hannah, Jasmin and Georgie were already there, sitting on a bench under the trees. They were sharing a family-sized bag of crisps and amusing themselves by pulling stupid faces, taking pictures of each other with their mobiles and then screaming with laughter when they checked the results.

'Settle down now, children,' I called with a grin as Chelsea and I went up to them. Chelsea had spotted the girls from way off and was going mad trying to pull the lead out of my hand. She'd almost yanked my arm off. 'Hi, y'all.'

'Hi, Chelsea.' Jasmin jumped off the bench and

got down on her knees to hug her. Hannah, Georgie and Grace crowded round to have a stroke and a pet too. Chelsea looked blissfully happy and her tail wagged non-stop.

'How about a *Hi, Lauren, how are you?*' I remarked drily, bending down to let Chelsea off her lead. She shot off immediately, nose to the ground, to investigate some bushes nearby.

'Oh, yeah, sorry, almost forgot about you there, Lauren,' Georgie replied, smirking. I pulled a cross-eyed face at her and she took a photo of me in close-up with her phone.

'*Very* flattering. Not!' Georgie remarked, showing me the picture. 'I think I might blackmail you, Lauren. You can afford it.'

'Katy not coming?' Jasmin asked as we settled ourselves on the bench again.

I shook my head. 'She didn't say why, though.'

'She never really does,' Jasmin grumbled. 'I miss her when she's not here. It feels all *wrong* when there's just five of us instead of six.'

'Katy hasn't missed any of our games since she started with the Stars, though, has she?' Grace pointed out. 'She's totally reliable.'

'She loves her footie, that's why,' Georgie chipped

in. 'She's a fantabulous defender too. If only she'd joined us at the beginning of the season, we might have got a promotion after all.'

'Never mind, let's just hope we can *exterminate* the Blackbridge Belles on Saturday,' I said in a dalek-type voice.

The others laughed.

'Yeah, we don't want another draw like our last match in December,' Georgie agreed.

'I don't really get why the Stars and the Belles are such big rivals,' Hannah said curiously. 'Don't forget, this'll be the first time I've ever played against them.'

'Oh, they're our *biggest* rivals!' Jasmin said earnestly. 'We hate them. In a kind of nice way, of course.'

'It's just that they're the closest club to the Stars,' Grace explained. 'They're only a few miles down the road. I think that the teams might have poached players from each other in the past. Anyway, no one really knows why, but the Stars and the Belles just don't get on.'

'Is that red-haired striker still playing for them?' I asked, 'You know, the one who's built like a tank and plays like one too?'

'You mean Lucy Grimshaw.' Jasmin actually shuddered. 'Grim by name and grim by nature. She frightens me half to death. She looks like she could pick me up and snap me in half!'

'Yep, she's still there,' Georgie groaned. 'I might ask Freya if I can wear a suit of armour on Saturday. I'll need it with Lucy Grimshaw thundering into the penalty area towards me—'

'Excuse me!'

We looked round and saw a middle-aged woman with a black Labrador puppy on a lead. At least, I *think* it was a Labrador. Since I don't like dogs, I wasn't really sure which breed was which! Meanwhile, Chelsea was gambolling happily around them with that *Yippee, I've made some new friends!* look on her soppy face.

'Is this your dog?' the woman went on, frowning as she pointed at Chelsea. 'If so, could you get her under control, please? She's annoying Augustus.'

I stood up. 'Chelsea, come here,' I called.

Of course, Chelsea ignored me.

'*Chelsea!*' I yelled.

The woman shook her head in disgust as Chelsea continued to waddle around them, sniffing curiously at her puppy. Picking Augustus up, she tucked him under her arm and strode off. Feeling a bit embarrassed, I ran across the field towards Chelsea.

'Chelsea, you naughty girl!' I scolded as I got closer.

Tail wagging, Chelsea shot me a mischievous look and bounded off. I let out a groan and turned to the others.

'She thinks this is a game,' I sighed. 'Help me catch her, will you?'

'Sure thing.' Georgie jumped to her feet. 'How difficult can catching one little dog be?'

Answer: *very* difficult. We chased Chelsea all over the football field and finally managed to corner her near a tree. Then we spread out in a circle, trying to surround her. Chelsea stood there, ears cocked, staring at us with her big brown eyes.

'Right, and now we start to close in!' I whispered, moving forward slowly. 'One, two, three...'

Suddenly Chelsea ran towards Jasmin and dashed straight between her legs. Jasmin gave a shriek of surprise.

'She nutmegged you, Jas!' Hannah yelled between fits of giggles as Chelsea pranced triumphantly off across the field again. She headed straight towards a mum with a pushchair, who immediately speeded up to get away from her. I felt embarrassed yet again as the young woman glared at us.

'We need to try something else.' Grace turned to Jasmin. 'Any of those crisps left?'

Jasmin took the almost-empty packet of crisps out of her pocket and Grace shook a few crumbs on the ground.

'Come on, Chelsea,' she called.

Looking interested, Chelsea immediately rushed over and began hoovering up the crisps greedily. I sighed with relief as I clipped her lead firmly onto her collar.

'Thanks, guys.'

'*That's* why you need to get Chelsea trained, Lauren,' Grace said, a bit too sternly, I thought. 'At the moment she's a nuisance to other people *and* other dogs.'

'Fine,' I snapped, feeling very annoyed with Grace, but even more annoyed with myself. 'I don't need a lecture, OK?'

'I *wasn't* lecturing you,' Grace retorted. 'I just hate to see dogs that aren't being looked after properly by their owners.'

'What do you mean?' I demanded, beginning to seethe with fury. 'Chelsea's fed and taken for walks and she's got somewhere warm to sleep. I *do* look after her properly, thank you very much, Grace Kennedy—'

'*Milkshake!*' Hannah said firmly. 'Stop it, you two.'

'Yeah, united we stand against the Blackbridge Belles,' Georgie chimed in with a wink. 'Divided we fall! We can't afford to get into fights with the big match coming up on Saturday.'

I drew in a shaky breath. I knew I'd over-reacted a bit. 'Sorry, Grace.'

'Me too.' Grace slid her arm around my shoulders and gave me a squeeze. 'Mates again?'

I nodded. But after I'd said goodbye to the others and was on my way home again, I thought about what Grace had said. Secretly, I was afraid that she was right and that I *wasn't* being very good to Chelsea. That made me feel very guilty. OK, so I had no intention of handing Chelsea over to just anyone – her new owner would have to prove to me that they'd look after her properly. But was I looking after her properly myself? According to Grace, I wasn't.

'Don't worry, Chelsea,' I murmured as we wandered home, 'I'll make sure you get *the* best owner in the whole world.'

Chelsea gave a little yap and went back to sniffing her way from lamp-post to lamp-post. Dad had spoken to all the local animal charities, and Mum had taken snaps of Chelsea on our digital camera to send to them, and to all the vets' surgeries in Melfield too. I'd tied a red ribbon around Chelsea's neck for the pictures, and she'd kept trying to pull it off with her teeth. It was *sooo* funny – even Tanya was laughing by the end of the photo session.

We were only five minutes from the house when I got a text from Katy, apologising for not being able to make it tonight because of 'family stuff'. So I gave her a call.

'Oh, hi, Lauren. So, did I miss anything?' Katy wanted to know.

'Not much,' I replied. 'Chelsea ran off and annoyed a dog called Augustus and then chased a mum with a push-chair, and we couldn't catch her except by setting a trap with crisps. Then Grace and I had a bit of a row because she told me off for not taking Chelsea to dog-training classes. That's about it.'

Katy laughed. 'And how are things with you?' she went on. 'How are you getting on with Tanya?'

'Um – not too well.' The words popped out of my

mouth before I could stop myself. 'Anyway, it doesn't matter,' I went on quickly. 'I think she might be leaving very soon anyway.'

'Really?'

There was silence. If anyone had asked me, I would have said that I knew Katy slightly less well than any of the other girls because she was such a private person. But now I just felt like pouring it all out to her. I longed to tell her about Tanya, and how much I hated my parents being away so much and all my secret fears that – well – maybe my mum and dad just didn't *want* to be at home with me.

'Oh, we'll see... Are you looking forward to the game on Saturday, Katy?'

The moment passed and then, you guessed it, I was kicking myself yet again for not opening up. But a girl's got her pride, you know. I was used to the others envying me and I didn't want them to start pitying me instead.

Why am I so stupid?

'OK, team talk!' Georgie yelled, striding into the middle of the changing-rooms. 'Gather round and listen up!'

All eleven of the Springhill Stars first team,

including me, rushed to join her. The match against the Blackbridge Belles was just about to start, and we were all hyped up to the eyeballs. It was an away game, and we were playing on the Belles' patch at the Blackbridge community centre. That meant we were at a bit of a disadvantage.

Dad had gone to France yesterday morning, but Mum was coming to the match like she'd promised. I'd pouted and moaned a bit when she'd told me she had to pop to the office first, but she'd promised me *faithfully* that she'd be there for the kick-off. She'd asked Jasmin and her mum to pick me up and bring me to the game because Tanya had gone shopping. We'd left Chelsea shut up in the kitchen with plenty of toys to keep her occupied. She'd fallen asleep almost straightaway, though, after her walk. I'd had a bit of a break this week because Dad had started taking Chelsea out on school mornings, which was nice of him! There'd been no news yet of Chelsea's owner coming to claim her, but I didn't care. The longer she stayed, the more likely Tanya was to get fed up and leave.

'Ooh, is this our team hug?' Jasmin asked, slinging her arms around me and Hannah, who were standing next to her.

'No, forget the huggy-huggy stuff today.' Georgie glared sternly at her. 'We need to go out there and show the Blackbridge Belles what's what!' She broke off and glanced at Grace. 'Er – Grace, do you want to do this? You're the captain, after all.'

'No, you go right ahead, Georgie,' Grace said with a shrug. 'You're much more terrifying than I am.'

'Hear, hear!' Jo-Jo and Ruby sniggered.

'OK, the Belles play hard and fight to the death,' Georgie went on earnestly. 'Watch out for that girl on the right, their captain, Jacintha Edwards. She looks like butter wouldn't melt, and the refs fall for it every time, but she's a hard nut. And then there's the human tank, Lucy Grimshaw—'

There were loud groans from everyone.

'Just do your best to keep her away from me, OK?' Georgie said with a wink. 'Let's go – and good luck out there!'

Whooping and slapping each other on the back, we headed out, just as the Belles came out of their own changing-room. I nudged Hannah and Katy.

'*That's* Lucy Grimshaw,' I whispered, pointing at a tall girl with long red hair and broad shoulders as she clattered out onto the pitch ahead of us.

'*Eek!*' Hannah gasped, 'She's big, isn't she? Are you sure she's not someone's mum in disguise?'

'She looks like she wears size-ten boots!' Katy murmured, eyeing Lucy's enormous feet.

'Just make sure you jump out of the way if she takes a shot at goal,' I advised them both with a grin as we ran outside, 'or you could get your head taken off!'

As we warmed up on the pitch, I looked around eagerly for Mum. I was absolutely *convinced* she wouldn't let me down today.

I never learn, do I?

Mum wasn't there. I looked around the touchline again and again at the groups of parents standing there, but I couldn't see her. I can't even explain how disappointed I was.

And then I saw someone else.

TANYA!!!

Anger boiled up inside me. Immediately I ran over to her, ignoring the ref, who was telling us to get into position for kick-off.

'What are *you* doing here?' I demanded rudely.

'Please don't speak to me like that, Lauren,' Tanya said, looking annoyed. 'Your mum rang me and asked me to come. She's been delayed at the office and—'

'Oh, right, I might have guessed!' I hissed at her. 'Look, why don't you just get lost and go back to your shopping or whatever you were doing? I don't *want* you here!'

'Lauren—' Tanya began.

'Oh, leave me alone!' I shouted.

Everyone was staring at us now, but I didn't care. I'd well and truly lost my temper, and I was burning up inside with fury and disappointment. Abruptly, I whirled round and ran to take up my position to get away from Freya, who was coming towards me, her face stern. Mum had *promised* me. Didn't that mean anything? I was gutted.

'Lauren, are you OK?' Jasmin asked nervously as I stomped past her.

'Well, obviously NOT!' I snapped. 'Leave me alone!'

I saw Jasmin, Hannah and Grace exchanging worried glances but I didn't care. I avoided looking at Freya too, who was hovering on the touchline near me. Hands on hips, I stood there waiting for the kick-off when all I wanted to do was run off and hide somewhere, *anywhere*.

As you can probably guess, the game didn't start so well for me. I took Jacintha Edwards down in the first couple of minutes with a bone-crunching tackle that had the ref racing over to have a word with me.

'Cool it, Lauren,' Freya called warningly.

'Shut up,' I muttered, but really low so that no one else could hear. I knew that Freya wouldn't take me off unless she had to because none of our subs were available today.

The Belles were getting most of the ball and the Stars were in total disarray, which I guess was all my fault. Every time I touched the ball, something seemed to go wrong.

We had a great chance to score when, after a mighty battle in midfield between Hannah and one of the Belles' defenders, Hannah came away victorious with the ball. Swiftly, she passed it to Emily, who went on a brilliant run towards the Belles' goal and into their penalty area. I was level, keeping pace with her, and she slotted the ball neatly across to me. All I had to do was get it in the net…

I tried to hit the ball as hard and as low as I could, but I accidentally sliced it. The ball flew up into the air and sailed over the crossbar.

'You idiot!' I groaned. My shot wasn't even close, and I was *so* angry with myself. What a great chance to take the lead wasted! But, the way I was feeling,

I don't think I could have scored today if everyone else had gone home and I was left with an empty goal.

I was so furious and frustrated, my play got even worse. I lost every ball I went for. I kept tripping over my own feet, and I just didn't seem to have my usual pace. The Belles had sensed that something wasn't right with our team, and that gave them the confidence to push forward. Jacintha Edwards had already won the ball from me three or four times and as a direct result of my rubbish mistakes, Lucy Grimshaw had twice gone close to scoring.

But somehow we managed to keep the score at nil–nil for the first twenty minutes. Then, as the Belles swept forward yet again, Katy bravely stuck her leg out and took the ball off Lucy Grimshaw's toe for a throw-in to the Belles, deep in the Stars' half.

'Lauren!' Georgie yelled at me. I was sulking on the other side of the pitch as Jacintha Edwards hurried to take the throw-in. 'Get over here in the box and defend!'

God, I *hate* being told what to do! And the way I was feeling, I knew I was more likely to score an own goal than help the Stars out of trouble.

I thought about ignoring Georgie, but I could feel Freya's eyes boring into my back, so reluctantly I went into our penalty area. There was a ruck going on, and everyone was jostling each other. Katy was marking Lucy Grimshaw and I hovered near her too, just in case Katy needed a bit of help.

I *think* Lucy saw that I was there, out of the corner of her eye. But suddenly she stepped backwards and trod on my left foot. She nearly crushed my toes with those gigantic boots of hers, I can tell you.

I yelled out in pain, but Jacintha was just taking the throw-in and everyone's eyes were on her.

I was *so* mad, I can't tell you. That red mist was up, and I was now gunning for Lucy Grimshaw. As the ball flew towards us, Katy, Lucy and I jumped for it, and so did everyone else in the box. Then I pushed Lucy in the back, hard.

I *swear* I didn't mean for this to happen. Lucy tumbled over and knocked straight into Georgie, who'd gone up for the ball too. Georgie gasped as Lucy cannoned into her and sent her flying. Then there was a loud thud as Georgie crumpled awkwardly to the ground, crying out in pain.

'Oh God!' I gasped, as the ref blew his whistle.

Freya immediately came flying onto the pitch, followed closely by Mr Taylor, Georgie's dad. I felt utterly sick with guilt and worry as both teams gathered around the goalmouth.

'Don't panic!' Georgie sat up, but she still looked a bit dazed. 'I'm fine. Just turned my ankle, I think.'

She climbed heavily to her feet, helped by Freya and her dad. But we could all see that her left ankle was hurting when she put her weight on it.

'Is it bad, Georgie?' Freya asked. I swallowed hard. What if Georgie's ankle was broken? It would be all my fault.

Georgie shook her head. 'It's just a sprain,' she replied, moving her foot gingerly.

But Mr Taylor still looked worried. 'Maybe I'd better take you to A&E,' he suggested.

'For a sprained ankle?' Georgie scoffed. 'No way, Dad. And besides, I want to play for the rest of the match.'

'Not a chance, my darling.' Mr Taylor tried to pick Georgie up in his arms, and she gave a squeal of protest. 'I'm taking you home.'

'Dad, I can walk!' Georgie protested, wriggling free. 'And I'm *not* going home – even if I can't play, I want to see the end of the game!'

I watched Georgie hobble from the pitch with her dad. Someone had rushed into the community centre and brought a chair out for her and she sat down, still looking a bit pale. I wasn't sure if Georgie or anyone knew that it was all my fault, though. Maybe I should just keep quiet…

'You shouldn't have done that, Lauren,' Jasmin muttered. Her normal happy, smiley face was angrier than I'd ever seen before. 'I *saw* you push Lucy into Georgie!'

'So did I,' Ruby agreed, and Alicia and Katy nodded.

I flushed with shame.

'I didn't *mean* to—' I began as the other Stars stared at me in dismay.

'Let's discuss this later,' Freya cut in firmly. 'One of you will have to go in goal for the rest of the match. Any volunteers?'

There was silence. I knew I ought to put my hand up, but all I wanted to do at the moment was dig a deep hole and jump inside it out of sight.

'I'll do it,' Hannah said quietly. Without looking at me, she trudged over to the goal and took up her position. Silently we all moved away, and the game re-started.

Hannah did her best, but she was no goalie, and we didn't have a chance after that.

Lucy Grimshaw scored the Belles' first goal just four minutes later.

We ended up losing 7–0.

CHAPTER SEVEN

It took a real effort for me not to burst into tears as the Stars walked despondently off the pitch at the end of the game. My face ached and my throat hurt as I tried to hold back the sobs. This was totally my fault. And after all that, my mum hadn't even turned up at the game, and now it was over. How *bad* did I feel?

'Lauren, a word,' Freya said sternly as the others went on down the corridor to the changing-rooms without speaking. Despite protests from her dad, Georgie had insisted on limping across to join us as we came off the field.

I hung back, my face burning with embarrassment.

'Do you want to tell me what happened out there today, Lauren?' Freya asked, raising her eyebrows.

'Not really,' I muttered. I stared down at my boots, which were all blurry because of the tears in my eyes. 'I just lost my temper, that's all.'

'And not for the first time,' Freya said drily. 'Is it true what Jasmin said, that you pushed Lucy Grimshaw into Georgie?'

I nodded. 'I didn't mean to—' I began and then I broke off and began to cry.

'Here.' Freya handed me a tissue from a pack in her pocket, and her voice was less stern as she went on, 'Lauren, you're a lovely girl, but you really *must* learn to control that temper of yours. It's going to get you into serious trouble one of these days.'

'Sorry,' I mumbled, wiping my face.

'I think there's someone else who deserves an apology more than me, don't you?' And Freya put a hand briefly on my shoulder before walking back out onto the pitch.

My heart sank to absolutely rock-bottom at the thought of facing Georgie. I didn't think she'd seen what happened, but one of the others would have told her by now. If ever there was a time to confess to my team-mates what had been going on in my life for the last few weeks and why I was in such a hopeless state, it was now...

My heart thundering with anxiety, I opened the changing-room door. Hey, I wasn't expecting balloons and banners, but neither was I expecting the hostile looks I got from *everyone* in there, including Jasmin, Hannah, Katy, Grace and Georgie.

I took a deep, shaky breath. 'Look, guys, I—'

'That has to be one of the most stupid and idiotic things you've ever done, Lauren!' Georgie yelled. She got awkwardly up from the bench and kind of *hopped* furiously towards me. It would have been funny if the whole situation hadn't been so tense. 'Lucy Grimshaw could have put me in hospital! Do you have *any* working brain cells, or do you just not think about anyone but yourself?'

'Georgie—' I began. But I'd forgotten *just* how bad Georgie's temper could be. Maybe worse than mine even. She stood there, giving me the evil eye, and completely *ripped* into me.

'You lost us the game today because of your childish and immature behaviour, Lauren Bell! You were completely selfish, as usual, and I hope you're pleased with yourself—'

'Hold on a minute, Georgie!' I broke in sharply. Whoa! Now I wasn't just upset, I could feel anger firing up inside me. 'What do you mean I was completely selfish *as usual*? I'm not selfish at all!'

'Oh no?' Georgie snapped. 'You're telling me you're not a spoilt, selfish little rich girl who never thinks about anyone else at all?'

That hit me like a slap in the face. I glared at Georgie as if I hated her, and at that very moment, I did. I was *so* furious, I couldn't think of anything to say at all.

'Georgie, Lauren, stop this now,' Grace chipped in.

'Yes, this isn't helping—' Hannah began.

'Don't worry,' I retorted, slamming my locker door open and grabbing my sports bag. 'I'm out of here!'

And the next second I *was* out of there. Still wearing my muddy Stars kit and football boots, I ran down the corridor. I was absolutely *fuming*. Whatever I'd done, Georgie had no right to speak to me like that! I didn't think I was spoilt or selfish – why did the other girls assume that just

137

because my parents were well-off, my life was perfect? It *wasn't!*

Tanya was waiting in the small car park at the side of the community centre for me. She raised her eyebrows when she saw that I was still wearing my dirty kit, but she didn't say anything, even when I climbed into the back of the car and sat down.

We drove home in silence. I could just see Tanya's profile from the corner of the back seat, and she looked nervous and miserable. I guess it couldn't be much fun for *her*, living with the Bell family at the moment, I acknowledged reluctantly. But that was exactly what I'd been hoping for, wasn't it? When Tanya had gone, Mum and Dad would *have* to take a bit more notice of me...

Mum's car was parked in the drive when we got home. I jumped out of the Mini, slamming the door with a crash that must have made Tanya wince. Then I marched into the house.

Mum hurried out of the study as I was unlocking the door. She looked very guilty, I was glad to see.

'Lauren, I'm *so* sorry—'

'You *promised* me, Mum!' I yelled. 'Where were you?'

'Lauren, please don't shout at me,' Mum said

firmly as Tanya came in and slipped off to the kitchen without a word. 'There was a very bad accident on the ring road near the office. There was a traffic jam and everything on that side of town came to a complete standstill for half an hour. By the time we started moving again, it was too late for me to get to the game.'

'If you hadn't gone to the office in the first place, you wouldn't have got stuck in the traffic jam!' I pointed out furiously. 'That's all you and Dad ever do – work, work, work!'

Mum looked even more guilty. 'Look, Lauren, I know I should have been at the match, and I'm so sorry, darling, but it simply wasn't my fault. How about you and I go shopping this afternoon? We can get those silver football boots you wanted—'

'I don't *want* to go shopping!' I snapped. 'I'm going to my room!'

And I pushed past Mum and ran upstairs. I could have screamed with frustration. Why couldn't Mum *see* that I didn't want endless presents, I just wanted a bit of time and attention? Did I really have to spell it out to her? Or did she just not *want* to see it?

I could hear Chelsea whining and scratching at my bedroom door as I ran along the landing. When

I went in, she hurled herself joyfully at me, wagging her tail so hard it looked like it might fall off. At least *somebody* loved me, I thought dolefully.

Full of self-pity, I curled up on my bed, settling Chelsea down beside me.

'Nobody understands, Chelsea,' I told her. '*Why* can't Mum and Dad just put me first sometimes, without me having to ask them?'

As I stroked Chelsea, I gradually began to calm down, bit by bit. *I shouldn't have lost my temper with Georgie*, I thought ruefully. I realised *now* that I should have let her rant and rave at me for a bit, and let her get it all out. Then I could have apologised properly, and we would have made up. But I just had to jump right in there, didn't I?

The thing that was worrying me most was that maybe Georgie and the others wouldn't want to be friends with me any more after this. That thought upset me more than anything. We had such a great time together when everything was going well. I couldn't bear to think that I was going to miss out on all that...

I started getting texts just as I was thinking of going downstairs to make Chelsea and myself some lunch. Jasmin's was first, swiftly followed by messages from Hannah, Katy and Grace. They all said pretty much the same thing. *Look, we can sort this out at training on Tuesday; Georgie'll calm down; don't worry, Lauren, it'll be OK...*

I felt a bit better, but not much. After all, Georgie was the only one who hadn't got in touch, and she was the one who mattered most. That obviously meant she was still mad at me.

I didn't reply to the texts, though. I didn't really know what to say except 'sorry'. And that didn't seem enough. First of all, I wanted to work out exactly how I was going to put things right. I thought about it for a while, and then I heaved Chelsea off my lap and, leaving her grumbling to herself on the bed, I went over to my computer.

I had an idea.

'Can't you put your foot down, Tanya?' I complained, as we drove towards Melfield College for Tuesday night training. 'I'm late as it is.'

'No,' Tanya replied calmly. 'There are speed cameras.'

Feeling annoyed, I poked my tongue out at the back of her head, and then I saw she was watching me in the driver's mirror. We were late because I'd lost Chelsea at the park again, and it had taken me ages to find her.

I slumped down sulkily in the back seat as the car crawled along, wishing I could get the next hour or so over with. Mum had gone away this morning to Edinburgh and would be home late on Thursday night. At least Dad was back from France, though. He was going to Brussels on Thursday morning, but it was only for one night. So at least I wouldn't be spending *too* much time alone with Tanya this week. We hardly even spoke to each other these days, and Tanya looked permanently depressed. Well, if she was *that* miserable, why didn't she just leave?

I hadn't seen any of the others since the disastrous match against the Belles on Saturday, although Hannah, Grace, Jasmin and Katy had kept in touch by text. I still hadn't heard from Georgie, though. I'd picked up my phone about a *million* times to send her a message. But I'd chickened out every time because I couldn't decide what to say. It would be best to speak to her in person. Tonight. If I *ever* got to training, that is…

I peeped inside the carrier bag lying next to me on the seat. I had a surprise for Georgie, and it would make everything OK, I hoped.

We finally pulled into the college car park ten minutes after the training session had started.

'I shall wait here for you, Lauren,' Tanya said coolly, taking a magazine from the glove compartment.

I didn't even bother to reply as I climbed out of the car, the surprise for Georgie in one hand and my sports bag in the other. I rushed into the college, through the groups of people arriving for their evening classes, and into the changing rooms. Grace had texted to let me know that Georgie's ankle had healed pretty fast and that she'd probably be at training tonight with the rest of us, although she'd be taking things easy.

Three minutes later I was running out onto the pitch. Freya had everyone, including Georgie, doing shooting drills, kicking five footballs into the net one after the other between a line of cones.

I felt very awkward and embarrassed because everyone stared at me as I joined them.

'Good to see you, Lauren,' Freya said warmly. 'You can join Team A. You're taking the shots at the moment.'

I lined up behind Jasmin, who looked a bit embarrassed, but she gave my arm a quick pat and smiled at me. Team B, Georgie's team, were collecting the balls that went astray before they took their turn at trying to score. Georgie was still hobbling slightly, and the others on her team, Grace, Jo-Jo, Hannah, Alicia and Emily weren't allowing her to run around too much.

I stared at Georgie until I caught her eye. She shrugged slightly and then she smiled at me, a bit reluctantly. I felt a wave of relief. I hoped things were going to be OK – especially when she saw what I'd got for her!

After the training session finished, I hung back a bit, pretending I needed to speak to Freya as the others went into the changing-room. To be honest, I still felt *very* uncomfortable. There hadn't been much time to talk to the others during the session, but now I was going to *have* to sort everything out.

'Come on, Lauren.' Hannah appeared beside me and slipped her arm through mine. 'Get it over with. Things will be a lot better, then.'

'I know,' I murmured as we went over to the door. Grace was holding it open, smiling, and Jasmin and Katy were hovering just inside the corridor, waiting for us. But they all looked a little embarrassed, and there was an awkwardness between us that hadn't been there before, even when we hardly knew each other. That upset me because I knew it was my fault. I *had* to put things right.

'Georgie's calmed down a lot now,' Jasmin told me as we went towards the changing-rooms. 'You're quite safe, Lauren!'

I managed a smile as we all went inside. Georgie was chatting to Alicia and Emily and didn't once look my way, which I'm sure was deliberate. Anyway, I got changed swiftly and silently, and then I knew I had to bite the bullet. I took the plastic bag out of my locker and walked across the changing-room to Georgie. Silence fell, and all eyes were on me.

'Look, Georgie,' I began, 'I just wanted to say *sorry* about what happened on Saturday, and, well –' I thrust the plastic bag into her hand '– this is for you.'

Georgie had begun smiling a little when I started speaking, but then she frowned. Without saying anything, she opened the bag and pulled out the navy-blue and white Spurs sweatshirt I'd bought for her. I'd got it online and I'd even paid extra to have it delivered express so that I'd have it for tonight. Knowing what a mad Spurs fan Georgie was, I was sure she'd *love* it.

Um – maybe I was wrong...

To my disappointment and alarm, Georgie was looking very embarrassed. Not only that, she looked – oh, I don't know. Not angry as such, just rather – *irritated*.

'Lauren, I can't take this,' she said abruptly. Rolling the sweatshirt into a ball, she shoved it back into the bag and then thrust it at me.

'Why not?' I said, probably a bit more aggressively than I should have done. But I couldn't see what the problem was, to be honest.

'It's too expensive—' Georgie began.

'Oh, don't be daft, Georgie,' I broke in. 'It didn't cost much. And anyway, my parents give me a *huge* allowance every month. I can afford it.'

Georgie was smiling now in a kind of cynical way. It totally got my back up. Especially as everyone else in the changing room looked completely embarrassed. 'Yeah, I'm sure,' she said sarcastically. 'We all know how rich your folks are, Lauren. You don't need to ram it down our throats the whole time.'

'You can't *buy* friendship, Lauren, however rich you are,' Hannah said quietly. 'It doesn't work that way.'

'I wasn't!' I retorted. 'And anyway, Jasmin gave Katy that new watch a few weeks ago, remember? What's the difference?'

'Hey, don't drag me and Katy into this!' Jasmin said with a frown.

'Lauren, Jasmin had *broken* my old watch, so it was just a replacement,' Katy snapped, looking very annoyed. 'I wouldn't have accepted it otherwise.'

'You must see the difference, Lauren,' Grace added quietly.

I stared angrily at Grace and the others. They'd moved to stand near Georgie, almost as if they were showing me that they were on her side, not mine. *Was* I trying to buy their friendship? The thought reminded me painfully of my mum and dad buying me stuff all the time to make up for them not being around. Suddenly I felt sick to my stomach.

'Oh, you lot are making such a fuss about *nothing*!' I said sharply, trying to hide the hurt I was feeling. 'It's just a cheap old sweatshirt, that's all. And I wish you'd all stop going on about how rich my parents are – I think you're just jealous!'

Grabbing my bag, I walked out of the changing room. I thought someone might call out to me or run after me, but they didn't...

Why couldn't I do anything right? I wondered as I trudged miserably to the car park where Tanya was waiting. I'd had enough of *everything*. Of Mum and Dad, of Tanya, and most of all, of the Springhill Stars. If Georgie, Grace, Hannah, Jasmin and Katy thought I was trying to *buy* their friendship, then I wanted nothing more to do with any of them.

As soon as I got home, I would ring Freya and tell her that I was leaving the team.

CHAPTER EIGHT

I felt exhausted and emotional by the time Tanya and I had driven home in silence. But I hadn't changed my mind. I couldn't be part of the Springhill Stars any longer. It was the perfect time to leave, too, with only one match away against the Turnwood Tigers next Saturday before the season ended.

Gran's little silver car was parked on the drive as we pulled up outside the house. As I climbed out of the Mini, she opened the door. Immediately Chelsea shot out like a bullet from a gun and flew towards me, barking a welcome.

'Hello, girl,' I said, grabbing her collar before she had a chance to take off down the drive. Chelsea danced around me, jumping up at my legs, looking utterly ecstatic that I was home at last. I felt a little comforted by that, even though I was still knotted up with misery inside.

'Lauren, you look very pale,' Gran said anxiously, drawing me into the warm, brightly lit hall. 'All that running around at your football training must have been too much for you—'

'Gran, I'm *fine*,' I broke in irritably. 'Where's Dad?'

'He's just popped out to get some petrol for his trip to the airport,' Gran replied. She frowned down at Chelsea, who was sitting at my feet chewing the fringes of the hall rug. 'Chelsea, stop that!'

To my surprise, Chelsea stopped immediately.

'I think she gets a bit bored when you're not here, darling,' Gran said to me. 'Maybe you should think about getting her a few more toys to play with. Although she may not be here much longer, anyway. Your dad had a call from one of the local vets today where he left Chelsea's photo, and—'

'*What?*' I wasn't at all prepared for the horrible, cold feeling of dread which flooded through me.

Tanya, who'd just come into the house, stopped in the hallway and looked at Gran enquiringly.

'Well, they think they might know who Chelsea's owner is,' Gran went on. 'That's good news, isn't it, darling?'

I was silent. *Why did I feel so upset?* It was only because I'd argued with the other girls and was leaving the team, that was all, I told myself. I'd grown used to having Chelsea around but I always knew she'd be going to a different owner eventually, one way or the other. I glanced down at Chelsea, who was now lying on my feet playing with the laces of my trainers. OK, I had to admit it, I'd miss her. Just a little.

I knew Tanya would be pleased. But she didn't say anything. Looking pale and tired herself, she disappeared into the kitchen.

'I know what you need to perk you up, Lauren,' Gran said, unwinding my fluffy pink scarf from my neck as if I was five years old. 'A course of multivitamins. I've been a different woman since I started taking my vitamins every morning. My doctor says—'

At that moment the front door opened again and Dad came in, the evening newspaper under his arm.

'Hi there, sweetie.' He dropped a kiss on my hair and bent to pat Chelsea, who'd waddled over to say hello. 'Everything OK?'

'Fine,' I fibbed. 'Gran said someone rang about Chelsea?'

'Oh, that.' Dad slipped his jacket off. 'The vet just rang me on my mobile. False alarm. Chelsea isn't the dog they're looking for.'

Big relief! It meant that Chelsea would still be around for a while to help out with my campaign to Get Rid of Tanya.

Well, what did you *think* I meant?

And now I had to ring Freya and get that over with...

I went upstairs to my room with Chelsea galloping ahead of me. I couldn't help wondering if I was doing the right thing, even though I'd made up my mind that leaving the team was what I was going to do. The Stars had been a *big* part of my life for the last few years, even before I'd become friends with Katy, Georgie and the others. But now I felt like the odd one out, and it wasn't a nice feeling. I was the youngest of the group, and I stuck out like a sore thumb because my mum and dad were so much wealthier than the other girls' parents. I didn't like that at all. And now it seemed that the others didn't want to be friends with me, anyway...

I felt a bit teary as I went into my bedroom and closed the door. It had been fab for a while to be part of the gang, having great mates who loved football as much as I did. But now they'd pushed me out into the cold. I didn't want to think about the fact that a lot of this was *my* fault. If I'd just told everyone what was happening, and how I felt about Mum and Dad and Tanya, instead of trying to cover it up and pretend that nothing was wrong, then maybe I wouldn't be in this situation. But now it was too late...

Then my phone started beeping. I fumbled for it in my pocket, feeling suddenly hopeful as I stared at the display screen. I had two unread texts. One from Jasmin and one from Grace.

Maybe it *wasn't* too late after all?

Feeling a whole lot happier, I snuggled down on the bed with Chelsea and checked my mobile.

Jasmin's message read: *Georgie still mad!! But we can sort it out, u just need to say sorry, J x*

I frowned and looked at Grace's text. *Hi L, give G a chance to calm down and then you can apologise, u know what G's like! luv Grace x*

Apologise?!

Suddenly that red mist was dancing in front of my eyes again, and I was absolutely *fuming*. Why should I apologise to Georgie? I'd tried that once, and look where it had got me. OK, so it was *my* fault that Georgie had been injured, but I'd tried to make it up to her and got it had had thrown back in my face. *She* was the one who had a massive problem with how wealthy my parents were. I was SICK of it! If the other girls thought so much of Georgie and so little of me, then I was better off out of it...

I was so angry now that when two texts arrived, one immediately after the other, from Hannah and Katy, I deleted them both straightaway without reading them. They'd only be saying exactly the same thing as Grace and Jasmin, so what was the point? I stabbed viciously at my *Contacts* menu and hit Freya's number.

Then I waited.

I could hear Freya's phone ringing, and my heart pounded. I wasn't just giving up my friendship with the other girls by leaving the team, I'd be giving up the football I loved too. Although I could always find another club. Maybe I'd join the Blackbridge Belles! *Not funny, Lauren...*

'Hello, Lauren.'

'Hi, Freya.' I cleared my throat. How did I do this? There was no other way except to come right out with it. 'Well, I – er – I just wanted to let you know that, well – I've decided I'm leaving the Stars. Sorry.'

There was silence.

'Can I ask why, Lauren?' Freya said calmly. 'Is this something to do with the other girls?'

'I don't really want to talk about it,' I muttered. 'Look, Freya, I'll get my mum or dad to call you to make it official—'

'Just wait until the end of the season before you make a final decision, Lauren,' Freya urged me. 'I really need you for this Saturday's game against the Tigers. I don't know if we'll have any subs available.'

'No, Freya, I don't *want* to—' I couldn't face seeing the other girls even one last time. I just wanted to forget that all this stuff had ever happened.

'We'll be one short, if you don't,' Freya cut in. 'Come on, Lauren – for the team?'

I sighed. I'd always really liked Freya, and I didn't want to let her down. 'Well, all right – but I'm not coming to training on Thursday.'

'It's your call, Lauren,' Freya replied quietly. 'I just don't want you to throw away all your hard work this season for nothing. I'll see you Saturday.'

I rang off, still feeling angry but also shaky and tearful, and oh, just generally *rubbish*. Had I done the right thing? I wondered, as I began to calm down a little. When I was mad, I often did stuff that I totally regretted later. Well, if the other girls *really* wanted me to stay, I'd find out by their reaction to the news that I was leaving, wouldn't I?

My phone trilled to tell me I had another text, and I grabbed it eagerly.

Could it be from Georgie? I wondered. hope surging through me. Maybe she'd decided that she'd make the first move and apologise to *me...*

Want 2 come 2 tea @ mine 2moz after school? Choc cake and ice cream on offer! Flo coming too! Daisy x

I sat staring at the text for a few minutes. Maybe I *should* spend more time with my non-footballing friends, I thought. And at least Flo and Daisy wouldn't keep going on about how rich my parents were. Their families were both well-off. Flo's had even more money than mine, *and* a bigger house. I didn't feel like the odd one out when I was with them. Flo and Daisy were always asking me to go horse-riding or to ballet classes, too. I'd talk to them about it tomorrow. Maybe it was time I found out who my *real* friends were...

'Surely you don't expect me to get on *that*?' I whispered fearfully to Flo and Daisy. Standing in front of us was this *huge* creature with big teeth, a long swishy tail and an evil gleam in its eyes. A horse (and his name was Henry). *EEK!*

It was Thursday evening and instead of going to train with the Stars, I was at the stables with Flo and Daisy, ready for my first horse-riding lesson. Don't ask me why! Daisy and Flo had talked me into it when we had tea together yesterday, and Dad had booked the lesson before he left for Brussels. He'd looked a bit surprised when I'd told him I was giving up football, but luckily he'd been too distracted preparing for his trip to question me too closely. And Gran, who'd popped round with a family-sized bottle of multivitamins for me, had been absolutely delighted, of course.

I hadn't texted Grace, Hannah, Jasmin or Katy back. I'd had some more messages asking if I was OK and saying that we could sort everything out at training tonight. *Yeah, right.* What they meant was that I had to apologise to Georgie and hope that she'd graciously forgive me and not bite my head right off. I hadn't had a single text from her, so I guessed she was still mad at me. I wondered what the girls would do when I didn't turn up for training, and Freya told them that I was leaving the team after the final game. Would they even care? I was beginning to doubt it. Georgie would probably be pleased, I thought, biting my lip. I was now beginning to regret giving in to Freya and agreeing to play the last match of the season. It was going to be *really* awkward on Saturday…

'Come along, Lauren.' Greta, who was giving me the lesson, looked at me expectantly, as she held the horse's reins. She was big and blonde with a no-nonsense manner that scared me just a little. Greta looked like she could tame a wild horse simply by *staring* at it. 'Let's practise mounting and dismounting, then. Remember what I told you?'

'Er – could Flo or Daisy show me one more time?' I asked hesitantly. My mates had kindly offered to hang around and help me for a bit, instead of going off for a ride on their own horses, and I was really grateful. I stared at Henry, who blew loudly through his nose. I wasn't really sure what I was doing here, to be honest. But if Flo and Daisy loved riding so much, surely I ought to give it a go?

I watched as Flo put her foot in the stirrup (I think that's what it's called!) and swung herself smoothly into the saddle.

'Now it's your turn, Lauren,' Greta said, as Flo dismounted just as neatly.

I went over to Henry, who was standing there quite patiently. Then I put my foot in the stirrup.

'Wrong foot, Lauren,' Greta said briskly, 'How are you going to swing your other leg over?'

'Oh, *bum*!' I groaned, feeling all flustered. I tried to yank my foot out of the stirrup and ended up almost falling over backwards. I saw that Flo and Daisy were trying not to giggle, and I pulled a face at them. Quickly I stuck my other foot in the stirrup.

'Right, one, two, three – hup!' I muttered, swinging myself up. Suddenly I was on top of Henry's back. 'Hey, I did it! Yay, me!'

But that was only the start. *Heels down, knees bent, chest out! Sit up straight! Don't lean forward! Keep your hands still!* God, I was exhausted after the first five minutes!

After spending ages learning about posture and how to control the horse, eventually I was allowed to take Henry into the paddock and we walked and trotted for a bit. Then the lesson ended. I dismounted awkwardly and thanked Greta, my legs wobbling like jelly. My bottom was completely throbbing too, and so sore, I didn't think I'd be able to sit down for a week!

Meanwhile, Flo and Daisy had gone off for a quick ride on their horses, Princess and Katrina, and then when they came back, they had to groom them using loads of different brushes and combs. Luckily I wasn't expected to groom Henry, but Flo and Daisy asked me if I wanted to help them, and as Tanya hadn't arrived to pick me up yet, I didn't have much choice. I kept well away from the back ends of Princess and Katrina, though!

By the time Mrs Rankin arrived to collect Flo and Daisy, I was *exhausted*. I felt as if I'd played three games in a row against the Blackbridge Belles.

'Lauren, are you sure you don't want a lift?' Flo asked as we left the stables.

'No, Tanya'll be on her way,' I replied absent-mindedly, as I checked my phone. Football training would be almost finished by now. Would

I get any texts from the girls when Freya told them I was leaving the Stars? Would they beg me to change my mind? Or wouldn't they care? I thought I could guess what Georgie's reaction would be…

'So, did you enjoy your first lesson, Lauren?' Daisy asked with a grin.

'I'll tell you when my bottom's stopped hurting!' I groaned, waving at Mrs Rankin. I was secretly convinced by now that horse-riding was not for me, but I didn't want to tell Flo and Daisy that after they'd been so kind. 'See you at school tomorrow.'

I leaned against the stable gates, wondering whether to text one of the others as Flo, Daisy and Mrs Rankin drove off. Grace, maybe. She was the oldest of all of us, and she was always good at sorting this kind of stuff out…

Oh, stop messing around, Lauren Melissa Bell, I told myself firmly. *You made your decision, now stick with it! If the other girls want you to stay in the team, they'll let you know…*

I was so deep in thought, I hadn't noticed that I'd been standing there for about twenty minutes. Suddenly I glanced at my watch and realised that Tanya was late. Where *had* she got to?

I hit speed dial and got through to Tanya's mobile,

but it went to voicemail almost immediately. I left a message and waited.

Another ten minutes went by and Tanya *still* hadn't turned up. I was feeling really irritated by now. The stables were just outside Melfield in the countryside, and it was too far for me to walk home. I tried my gran's home number and her mobile. She didn't answer either of them, so I just left messages.

I was just about to try my Auntie Rehana, when I saw a bus winding its way down the country lane where I was standing. The bus had *Blackbridge* on the front, and I knew I could walk from there and be home in about fifteen minutes. Luckily, I had some money on me. I made an instant decision and ran down the lane to the bus stop.

As I sat down at the back of the bus, I left more messages for Tanya and Gran, telling them that I was making my own way home. Then a sudden thought struck me. Mum and Dad wouldn't be at all pleased that Tanya had forgotten about me! Maybe they'd even give her the sack.

But things were about to get a whole lot worse...

When I got home, Tanya's car was parked on the drive. So she *had* forgotten about me, I thought.

Wait until I told Mum and Dad....

'Tanya!' I yelled, as I let myself into the house. 'Why didn't you come and collect me? I've had to get the bus!'

But the only sound I could hear was Chelsea, shut up in my bedroom, barking madly. Apart from that, the house felt silent and empty.

It was then that I began to feel extremely worried. *Where was Tanya?*

CHAPTER NINE

'Tanya!' I shouted again. Maybe she was up in the loft room at the top of the house, and she couldn't hear me.

I ran up the stairs. As I went past my bedroom, I opened the door and Chelsea barrelled out, panting loudly. Pausing just to give her a quick pat, I went up to the second floor and then climbed the steel spiral staircase to the loft extension.

The door was closed. I stopped outside, suddenly feeling a little awkward. I hadn't been anywhere near the loft since Tanya had moved in.

I tapped on the door, Chelsea sitting on

the staircase beside me.

'Tanya?'

No answer. I turned to go back downstairs, but then I wondered if maybe she'd fainted or was lying seriously ill in bed. So I reached for the door handle and went in.

The room was empty. It was tidy and the bed was made and there were no clothes lying around, but Tanya wasn't there. For a moment I wondered if she'd just taken her stuff and left without telling anyone, but there was make-up and a bottle of perfume on the dressing table.

As I turned to go, I noticed a photo in a wooden frame on the table by the bed. I was curious, so I went over to take a look. I know I shouldn't have been poking around, but, well, I did it anyway.

It was a picture of a girl about my age. She had long blonde hair and blue eyes and she was holding a tiny black kitten. The girl looked a lot like Tanya...

Suddenly my mobile phone rang out, shattering the silence. I gasped with fright and dropped the photo frame, which luckily landed on the bed.

With trembling hands, I grabbed my phone from my pocket. *Mum calling* flashed at me from the display screen.

'Hello, Mum?'

'Hello, darling,' Mum replied cheerfully 'Just to let you know I'll be back tonight as I said, but my plane's been delayed by around an hour or so. I'm at the airport now. Will you tell Tanya I'll be a little late back?'

'I will, if I can find her,' I replied. 'She didn't come to pick me up from the stables, and she's not in the house.'

I heard Mum's sharp intake of breath at the other end of the line. 'How did you get home, then?'

'I took the bus.'

'Did you try Tanya's mobile?' I could tell Mum was trying to control her anxiety, and her anger too.

'Yes, but it just keeps going to voicemail. I tried Gran, but she's not answering either.'

'Lauren, listen to me carefully,' Mum said urgently. 'Try Gran again, and if she's still not answering, then try Uncle Rob and Auntie Lucy, or Uncle Sam and Auntie Rehana. If *they* don't answer, then ring Jasmin's mum or Flo's or Daisy's. And if you can't get through to any of them—'

'Mum, it's OK, I get it,' I broke in. 'Don't worry, I'm a big girl now.' But I felt warmed by her obvious concern for me.

'I just don't like to think of you all alone in the house, darling,' Mum said a bit shakily.

'I'm not alone,' I reassured her, patting Chelsea, who was standing next to me. 'If anyone breaks in, Chelsea will see them off, no problem.'

'She's more likely to lick them to death,' Mum replied. 'I'm going to ring off now, Lauren, but I want you to call me the *second* you've spoken to someone. Promise?'

'Promise, Mum. Speak to you soon.'

I rang off. I was just about to hit speed dial to call Gran again, when I thought I heard the front door close downstairs. Chelsea immediately dashed out of the loft, so she must have heard it too. Was it Tanya? If so, she was in big trouble, judging from my mum's voice. I should have been delighted, and I sort of *was*. But I couldn't help feeling a bit worried. Tanya couldn't just have vanished into thin air...

I clattered downstairs after Chelsea. Gran was standing in the hallway, looking completely flustered.

'I only just got your voicemail about Tanya, darling, and I came straight round. I'm so glad you got yourself home safely. Is Tanya here?'

167

I shook my head. 'I've just phoned Mum to tell her.'

'Well, this is most unlike Tanya.' Gran looked both worried and annoyed. 'I wonder where she's got to?'

I took my phone out of my pocket to ring Mum back, as I'd promised. But before I could make the call, we heard a car turn into the drive and then pull up outside the house. Gran and I both ran to the door, and Gran opened it while I grabbed Chelsea's collar.

It was a police car. Gran and I both watched in disbelief as Tanya climbed awkwardly out of the back seat, helped by a policewoman. Her arm was in a sling, there was a bruise above one eye and she looked pale and fragile.

'Tanya!' I burst out, feeling suddenly very frightened, 'What happened?'

Gran had already run over to put her arm around Tanya, who looked ready to faint.

'I—' Tanya began weakly, but she couldn't say any more, and tears began to roll silently down her cheeks.

'Let's get Tanya inside first, shall we?' the policewoman said. 'Explanations can wait.'

My gran might be a bit of a fusspot, but she's a *fan-brill-tastic* person to have around if anyone needs looking after. In about two minutes flat, she had Tanya settled on the sofa against a pile of cushions, shoes off, and covered with a chocolate-brown cashmere throw. I sat down silently next to her with Chelsea at my feet. Meanwhile the two police officers followed us into the living room and sat down too.

'I'm afraid Tanya's had rather a nasty shock,' the policewoman told us. 'She's been mugged.'

'Mugged!' Gran and I both exclaimed in horror.

'I walked down to the local shops,' Tanya said faintly, 'and two boys on bicycles knocked me over and stole my bag.' She turned her head slightly to look at me. 'My mobile phone was inside, that's why I couldn't call you, Lauren. I'm so sorry—'

'It's OK,' I cut in quickly. 'I got the bus home. I'm fine.'

'You poor girl.' Gran patted Tanya's hand. 'Should we call the doctor?'

'We wanted to take Tanya to A&E to get her checked over,' the policewoman said, 'but she was anxious to get home—'

'I was very worried about Lauren,' Tanya broke

in, and I just felt so *bad*. 'I wanted to call, but without my phone, I couldn't remember the numbers...'

'Luckily it happened near the local surgery, so we took her in there and one of the nurses bandaged her up,' the policewoman went on. 'It's just a sprained wrist, nothing too serious.'

'We'll come back and take a statement tomorrow, when Tanya's feeling less shocked.' The male police officer stood up. 'You take it easy for now, Tanya.'

'Thank you, officers,' Gran said, 'I'll show you out.'

They went over to the door and Tanya lay back on the cushions, closing her eyes. Just then my mobile went off. I jumped up to follow the others out so it didn't disturb Tanya.

'...and she seemed really worried about losing her job here,' the policewoman was saying to Gran in a low voice. 'She was concerned because she's a single parent and is providing for her daughter, who still lives in Slovakia with Tanya's parents.'

'Her daughter?' Gran repeated in surprise. 'Tanya's never mentioned her.'

I realised that it must be the girl in the photo by the bed.

My phone was still ringing fit to bust. I sat down on the bottom of the stairs and pressed the answer button.

'Lauren, it's me again!' Mum said, sounding frantic with worry. 'I'm just about to get on the plane and you haven't called me back. What's happening, darling? Did you get through to Gran?'

'I'm fine, Mum,' I replied quickly. 'Gran turned up here the moment you rang off. And Tanya's back. She was at the local shops and she got knocked over and robbed—'

'What!' Now Mum sounded horrified. 'Is she OK?'

'She's hurt her wrist and she's got a few bumps and bruises. The two boys took her phone which is why she couldn't call me. She wouldn't let the police take her to hospital for a check-up because she was worried about me—'

I stopped suddenly. Why was I explaining all this? Was I trying to get Tanya off the hook? Well, I *was* only telling the truth, wasn't I? And to be honest, when I'd seen her getting out of the police car looking like death, I kind of couldn't remember why I thought I'd hated her for so long...

'Oh, poor Tanya!' Mum exclaimed. 'Give her my

best, won't you, Lauren, and tell her not to worry about anything. Look, darling, I'll be home tonight and you can tell me everything, then, all right? Love you.'

'Me too,' I replied.

The police had gone by now and Gran had hurried back into the living room to check on Tanya. Now she came out again as I stood up.

'I'm going to make Tanya a nice hot cup of sweet tea and a bowl of soup,' she said. 'Go and sit with her, will you, Lauren? I don't think she should be left alone just now.' Gran smiled at me. 'Although she's not *actually* on her own – someone's looking after her!'

As Gran went off to the kitchen, I realised that Chelsea hadn't followed me out into the hall. I left my phone on the hall dresser and went into the living room. There was Chelsea on the sofa, snuggled up next to Tanya. My eyes widened.

'Chelsea and I have become friends over the last few weeks,' Tanya explained quickly and a little nervously, as if she thought I was going to fly into a temper or something. 'She misses you when you're at school.'

I sat down next to them. I didn't know quite

what I was going to say to Tanya, but then it just popped out.

'Why didn't you tell us you had a daughter in Slovakia?' I asked curiously.

Tanya sighed. She was looking a little better now with a bit more colour in her face. 'I wasn't trying to hide it, Lauren,' she replied. 'It's just that – I miss Gabriela so much. It's easier not to talk about her...' Her voice trailed away.

'Is Gabriela the same age as me?' I asked, then blushed. 'Sorry, I saw her photo when I was looking for you earlier in the loft.'

'She is twelve next month.'

'Are you going home for her birthday?' I asked.

Tanya nodded. 'I have arranged with your parents to have some holiday time, so I can go back to Slovakia for one week.'

'And doesn't Gabriela *mind* you working away in England?' I asked curiously. I knew I was being nosey, but I couldn't help myself. I wanted to know.

'We have talked about it so many times, Lauren,' Tanya said with a shrug. 'Gabriela knows I'm doing this so that she can have a better life and a good education. Then *she* will not have to become a housekeeper in a foreign country, if she doesn't want to.'

'I see.' I bit my lip. I imagined what it would be like not to see my mum for months at a time, like Gabriela. And I thought *I* had it bad. Now I understood what Tanya had meant on that first morning when she'd said I was lucky…

'It's always better to talk about these things, Lauren,' Tanya said, as she gently stroked Chelsea's head. 'Your parents only want what they think is best for you, just like I only want what I think is best for Gabriela. But sometimes people forget to talk, or they're afraid to. And then everything becomes muddled.'

I was silent. I understood what Tanya was trying to say, in her quiet way. I smiled at her, and you know what? I think it was the first time I'd smiled at her since she arrived.

'Can we try to get along from now on, please, Lauren?' Tanya asked hesitantly. 'I would *really* like us to become friends.'

I was feeling very ashamed of myself by now. I couldn't trust myself to speak, so I simply nodded. We said nothing more then because Gran bustled in with a tray of tea and soup, and began fussing around Tanya. But I think we'd finally managed to sort things out.

Later, sitting in my room with Chelsea, I thought about what Tanya had said.

But sometimes people forget to talk, or they're afraid to. And then everything becomes muddled...

I knew that Tanya was right. I *would* talk to Mum and Dad and tell them how I was feeling. I should have done it ages ago.

But what about Hannah, Grace and the others? Maybe I should try to talk to them too. Even though I didn't really feel that I'd done anything wrong, maybe I *should* apologise to Georgie – or at least, talk things over with her. Then I wouldn't have to leave the Stars...

I took my phone off the hall dresser and stared at the display screen. I hadn't heard them arrive, but I had two missed calls, one voicemail message and four new texts. Quickly I scrolled through the list. They were all from the girls, but none of them was from Georgie. What a surprise. *Not*. The voicemail was from Jasmin, and I listened to that first.

'Hi, Lauren,' Jasmin gabbled breathlessly. 'We were all *really* gutted when Freya told us you were leaving the team! You've got to change your mind. We all want you to stay. Well, Georgie says she doesn't care one way or the other, but she doesn't *mean* it. We were trying to persuade her to text or call you, but she won't – you know what she's like! She just says you shouldn't have given her that sweatshirt and that she's not a charity case and she's sick of you flashing your cash, and I guess we kind of agree with her, but the rest of us would *really* like you two to make up so that everything can go back to how it was before—'

The voicemail cut off. I stood there staring at my phone, feeling more upset and hurt than angry. Jasmin was pretty dippy and she didn't always think about what she said before she said it. But it was clear that Georgie was still furious with me. She couldn't even be bothered to send me a text when she knew I was leaving the team for good. And after what Jasmin had said, knowing how much of this was all my own fault, I knew I couldn't face Georgie, or the others, on Saturday.

Swallowing hard, I hit speed dial and rang Freya's number. Her crisp, clear voice told me to leave a message and I was relieved, because I knew she'd try and talk me out of this. I was right, it was better to make a clean break of things immediately.

'Hi, Freya, it's Lauren. I've definitely decided that I'm leaving the team right now, so I won't be playing on Saturday against the Tigers. Thanks for everything. Bye.'

CHAPTER TEN

'Tanya looks much better today, doesn't she?' my mum remarked as she put the car in gear and pulled off the drive. It was the following morning, and even though Mum had got back late last night, she'd insisted on getting up to take me to school. 'What an ordeal for her, though.'

I nodded. 'I'm glad you're home again, Mum. And thanks for bringing that pressie for Chelsea. She loves it!'

Mum had come home and instead of bringing a present for me, she'd unexpectedly turned up with one for Chelsea. It was a big ceramic dog bowl in the shape of a bone that split into two halves, one for food and one for water. Chelsea had gone mad for it, and had spent half the evening pushing the bowls around the kitchen with her nose.

Mum looked a little embarrassed. 'Well, my plane was delayed so I had time to do a bit of shopping,' she replied. Then she glanced sideways at me. 'Are you OK, by the way, Lauren? You look pale, honey.'

I shrugged. I hadn't slept very well. Freya had tried several times to call me back, but I'd just cut the connection without speaking to her and also ignored her texts. She'd left me a voicemail, though.

'Hi, Lauren,' Freya had said calmly, 'I understand you're feeling upset at the moment, and I know the reason why. Grace has explained about what happened with Georgie. I'm going to call Georgie myself right now, and see if we can't sort this out. You're a good player, and it would be a disaster for the Stars to lose you. Will you have another think about it? Take care, Lauren. Bye.'

I'd got that message last night, and I *still* hadn't heard anything from Georgie. If even Freya couldn't persuade her, it was all over.

'Time to move on, Lauren,' I thought forlornly.

I guess I hadn't ever *really* believed that I'd end up

leaving the Stars. At the back of my mind I'd always secretly thought that everything would get sorted out, and we'd all live happily ever after. But it just hadn't worked out that way.

'Lauren?' Mum's voice broke into my thoughts and I realised I hadn't answered her question. 'Are you all right?'

'I'm OK, Mum,' I said quickly. 'Gran's got me rattling with multivitamins! But...' I hesitated, remembering my conversation with Tanya the previous night. This was going to be difficult, but it had to be done. 'I *do* want to talk to you.'

'I think I know what you're going to say, darling.' Mum stopped at a red light.

'You do?' I was surprised.

Mum tapped her manicured nails on the steering wheel, looking very serious. 'It's about me and your dad being away so much, isn't it?'

I nodded, feeling very relieved that Mum was making this easier for me.

'But how did you know?'

'Because I've been feeling a bit down about it myself,' Mum confessed. 'I was so thrilled when I got the job, I didn't really think about how much I'd have to be away from home. I miss you and your dad so much. And then yesterday when Tanya wasn't there and you were all alone and your dad and I weren't there, either—' Mum suddenly sounded all tearful and wobbly.

'Oh, Mum, I was *fine*,' I assured her. 'You were right, in one way. I'm old enough to look after myself, sometimes. But I just *wish* the three of us could hang out more together.' I took a deep breath. This was the difficult bit. 'To be honest, I've been kind of wondering if you and Dad even *want* to spend time with me at all.'

'Lauren!' Mum looked absolutely horrified. 'You mustn't ever think that, darling. You're the most important thing in our lives. Do you *really* feel that way?'

Sometimes,' I replied. 'You both work long hours, and you and Dad are always working at home too, when you're there, which isn't all that often—'

'I know, and I realise now that something needs to change,' Mum said, wiping her eyes. 'I'm going to talk to your dad when he gets home later this morning, and sort something out. I mean it, Lauren.'

'But how do I *know* that?' I burst out, longing to be convinced but not quite believing it could be quite as easy as that. 'You and Dad might try for a little while, but when your work gets busy, you'll forget all about me, and then it'll all start again.'

Mum bit her lip, looking guilty.

'You're entitled to feel that way, darling. I suppose our track record hasn't been that great.'

'I'm fed up with being passed around like a parcel to anyone who'll have me,' I muttered glumly. I was going to say that I'd like my parents to come to more of the Stars' matches, but I'd just remembered, with a sinking heart, that I'd left the team now.

'Lauren, your dad and I are going to try really hard to get a better work/life balance than the one we have now,' Mum promised in a very serious tone. 'Please trust us, darling. And if we slip back into our old ways, you have my permission to make a big fuss and yell at us very loudly! Deal?'

'Deal!' I said, feeling relieved, as we drew up outside Riverton. Flo and Daisy were waiting for me by the gates. At least this was all out in the open now, so I wouldn't be afraid of speaking up if I felt Mum and Dad were neglecting me a bit again because of work. 'I'll be keeping a close eye on you and Dad from now on, Mum! Oh, and thanks for offering to walk Chelsea this morning.'

'I'll take her out as soon as I get home,' Mum

promised. 'I could do with the fresh air and some time to think.'

We hugged each other extra-hard before I jumped out of the car. Things were starting to look up, I thought happily. Tanya and I had become closer, and Mum and Dad had realised that we needed more family time. The only big black cloud hanging over me was the fact that I'd left the Springhill Stars, and my so-called friends didn't seem to care that much...

I'm so *stupid*, though. I still kept checking my phone eagerly during break times and at lunch time. I guess I was hoping that I might get a make-up text from Georgie. But there was nothing. Grace, Jasmin, Hannah and Katy kept sending me messages urging me not to leave the team and to sort it out with Georgie. But they were all on Georgie's side, I knew, and what could I do, if Georgie refused to be mates any more? By the end of the day I'd decided that I would *definitely* start looking for a new club, ready for next season.

I just didn't think it would end like this, I thought miserably as Mum drove me home after school. *I mean, this is Georgie's fault too, not just mine. Oh, well, it's their loss...*

But even though I was putting a brave face on things, I knew that it was *my* loss too. We'd been having such a great time getting to know each other, and becoming closer. I imagined them all playing football and going round to each other's houses and going out for milkshakes and having a laugh together – but I wouldn't be there. They'd be five instead of six.

When we got home, though, I cheered up a little. Chelsea was crazy with joy to see me, as usual, and I popped upstairs to say hi to Tanya, who was resting in her room. Dad was back from Brussels, and he and Mum had obviously been having a serious talk about everything that had happened. The three of us (no, four – I forgot Chelsea!) sat down in the living room together, and Mum brought in some tea and cakes.

'Lauren, your mum's told me what you said this morning, and we've agreed that things have become a bit too hectic around here over the last few weeks.' Dad paused and yawned, rubbing his eyes. He looked very tired himself, I suddenly realised. 'So we're both going to try to work less at home. And that's a promise.'

'We're going to have lots more family time,' Mum

added. 'Times when we can all be together and do something fun.'

'Oh, that's cool!' I said eagerly. 'And we don't have to go out *every* time, do we? I mean, I *love* shopping, but it would be great if we could hang out at home sometimes just watching DVDs or playing board games or taking Chelsea for walks.'

'Sounds good to me,' Dad agreed with a smile. 'And talking of Chelsea...'

Chelsea had been wandering around the living room, sniffing at the skirting boards, but she stopped and pricked up her ears when she heard her name.

'Watch this,' Dad whispered. 'Chelsea – here, girl!'

To my surprise, Chelsea immediately trotted over to Dad.

'Sit!' Dad instructed her.

Chelsea sat, tail wagging. I couldn't believe it!

'Good girl.' Dad took a dog treat from his pocket and Chelsea gulped it down so fast, it hardly touched the sides.

'Dad, that's brilliant!' I gasped. 'Did you teach her that?'

Dad nodded, looking more pleased with himself

than if he'd just clinched a huge deal for his company! 'Yep, it's just a bit of basic training,' he replied. 'I used to have a dog called Barney when I was a boy.'

I remembered then that I'd seen old photos of Dad when he was a kid with a scruffy brown mongrel.

'Chelsea, you're so clever!' I got down on my knees and fussed her to bits. 'I think you deserve an extra-long walk as a reward.'

At the word *walk*, Chelsea dashed out into the hall and sat down expectantly by the coat-stand where we always hung her lead. Mum, Dad and I laughed.

'Are you OK to go alone, honey, or would you like some company?' Dad asked as I went to get my jacket.

'I'm fine on my own, Dad.' I replied. 'And you look tired, anyway.'

As Chelsea and I left the house, I was secretly wondering if Georgie, Grace and the others would be at the park tonight. That was why I'd refused Dad's offer and was keen to go alone. We quite often met up the evening before a match, either at the park or at someone's house, to discuss the Saturday game. But it didn't matter if they were in the park or not, did it, I told myself firmly. Even if I saw them, Georgie wouldn't be speaking to me, anyway. We'd probably just ignore each other...

As Chelsea and I walked towards the park gates, I glanced nervously up and down the street to see if the others girls were around. They weren't, but I *did* see Flo and Daisy. They were walking towards me, and Daisy had her spaniel puppy, Coco, with her on a lead. They didn't see me because they were deep in conversation.

I admit it, I looked down at Chelsea and I panicked. I dived through the park gates as fast as I could, pulling Chelsea with me. Quickly, I looped her lead through the fence railings and left her there. I hated myself for doing it, but I was still embarrassed at the thought of introducing Chelsea to my school friends. Then I hurried back out of the gates again. Had Flo and Daisy seen us?

The girls were wandering along on the opposite side of the road, still chatting. Then Flo glanced up and saw me.

'Hey, Lauren!' she called. 'What are *you* doing here?'

'Oh, I'm meeting my football mates in the park,' I fibbed, hurrying across the zebra crossing towards them. Coco was pulling at her lead to get to me, and I bent down to stroke her. I'd met her before at Daisy's house and she *was* gorgeous – tiny and cuddly, with a thick amber and white furry coat, long silky ears and melting chocolate-brown eyes. Chelsea would look even uglier next to her.

'I thought you told us at school today that you'd left the Springhill Stars?' Daisy said, looking surprised.

'Er – I have,' I replied awkwardly. I'd forgotten I'd told them that! 'I'm – er – still meeting my mates tonight, though.'

'So you're not playing in a match tomorrow?' Flo asked.

I shook my head.

'Why don't you come to our dance school and watch a few ballet classes tomorrow, then?' Daisy invited me. 'You never know, you might find yourself a whole new hobby!'

'OK,' I said with a shrug. Well, why not? There's no reason why a footballer can't do ballet, is there? Although somehow I couldn't see Cristiano Ronaldo or Wayne Rooney in a tutu!

'My mum usually takes us,' Flo said, 'So we could pick you up on the way – about eleven o'clock?'

'Fine,' I agreed. 'Er – are you and Coco going to the park?'

Daisy shook her head. 'Coco gets too nervous because of all the other dogs,' she replied. 'We're just going to walk her around the streets.'

Feeling relieved, I waved at Flo, Daisy and Coco as they went off. But I knew I couldn't carry on like this for ever. Sometime very soon I was going to have to make a decision about what was going to happen to Chelsea...

But maybe Chelsea had already made that decision for me.

Because, when I ran back into the park, Chelsea was gone.

I stood there staring in disbelief at the spot where I'd tied her up.

'Chelsea?' I called, looking around. I expected to see her come waddling out of the bushes. But she didn't. 'Chelsea!' I called, more loudly.

I ran around, looking behind trees and under bushes, but there was no sign of her. I hadn't tied her lead tightly enough to the railings, I thought, wishing I'd been more careful. Chelsea must have pulled herself free. I'd been in a hurry, too worried about whether Flo and Daisy had spotted us. But Chelsea couldn't have gone far. Could she?

I searched for another ten minutes and that was when I *really* started to panic.

The trouble was, the park was a big one, and it had at least five different entrance and exit gates leading out of it. Chelsea might already have gone out of any one of them, and a couple of them led onto a busy main road... I swallowed hard. Why hadn't Chelsea come to find me when she got loose? *Now* I realised that I wouldn't have cared if Flo and Daisy thought Chelsea was ugly, as long as she was safe. But there were too many interesting smells and people and dogs to investigate in the park, and Chelsea had obviously got distracted and gone off on her own.

My heart thumping with fear, I ran down the path that led towards the football field. I was calling Chelsea's name and looking all around me, but there was still no sign of my little dog.

It was then I remembered, with a terrible, sinking feeling, that I hadn't even bothered to write our address and phone number on Chelsea's collar. There was a tag hanging off the collar with a tiny piece of paper inside for just that reason, but I just hadn't got around to it. I'd been lazy and now Chelsea was lost and I might never see her again and it was all my fault—

'Lauren?' said a familiar voice behind me. 'Are you OK?'

CHAPTER
ELEVEN

I spun round. I'd thought I was hearing things, but there was Jasmin. She was standing right behind me. Grace, Hannah, Katy and Georgie were with her. I stared at them in disbelief and then I just burst into tears.

Immediately Jasmin, Grace, Katy and Hannah gathered around me. Georgie, though, stayed a short distance away, a stern, unsmiling look on her face. Jasmin gave me a hug and Hannah handed me a tissue from her pocket.

'Don't worry, Lauren, it's clean!' she said with a grin.

I felt a bit embarrassed as I gulped back my sobs.

'What are *you* guys doing here?' I asked shakily, mopping at my eyes.

'Now, come on, Lauren,' Grace said, shaking her head at me, 'You didn't think we were going to let you get away *that* easily, did you?'

'I don't know,' I mumbled, staring down at my feet.

'Well, we weren't getting very far with our texts and calls to you, Lauren,' Jasmin confided, 'so we were planning to do something at the match on Saturday and get you and this stubborn idiot –' she pointed at Georgie '– to sort things out face to face!'

'Oi!' Georgie snapped, glaring at Jasmin. 'Less of the name-calling, please!'

My heart plunged. It was obvious that Georgie *still* didn't want to make up, whatever the other girls said.

'When we found out you'd told Freya you're not playing tomorrow, we were hoping we'd find you at the park tonight walking Chelsea,' Katy chimed in. 'So here we are!'

'And if you *weren't* here, we were all going to turn up on your doorstep and beg you to come back to the team.' Hannah patted my shoulder.

'Even Georgie?' I asked a bit sarcastically, raising my eyebrows.

Hannah, Jasmin, Katy and Grace immediately turned to stare at Georgie.

'Leave me out of it,' Georgie muttered sulkily. 'They *forced* me to come with them tonight.'

'Oh, really, Georgie!' Jasmin exclaimed with a giggle, 'Has anyone in the history of the whole world *ever* made Georgia Taylor do a single thing that she doesn't *really* want to?'

A tiny smile tugged at the corners of Georgie's mouth, but she bit it back.

'Look, you all know Lauren shouldn't have pushed Lucy Grimshaw into me like that—' Georgie began, glancing at me.

'I know,' I broke in, 'but I *did* say sorry, if you remember.'

'And if anyone should understand about someone losing their temper and doing something silly,' Grace pointed out gently, 'it's *you*, Georgie.'

Georgie looked a bit taken aback by that. 'Anyway,' she went on, 'Lauren shouldn't have bought me that sweatshirt, either. I don't want charity.'

'No, you're a head case, not a charity case,

Georgie,' Hannah said. She had such a straight face that no one reacted for a moment, and then we all grinned, even Georgie.

'I never thought of it like that,' I told Georgie. 'I just felt so bad about what I'd done, saying sorry didn't seem to be enough. I didn't mean to make you feel that way, Georgie.'

Jasmin, Hannah, Grace and Katy all eyeballed Georgie.

'All right, all right!' Georgie said, looking a little embarrassed. 'I said some really mean things to you, Lauren, and I *am* sorry about that, but—'

Now that Georgie had actually apologised (a bit reluctantly, but it was still an apology!), I suddenly felt all emotional and tearful.

'I've been acting like an idiot for weeks because I've got stuff going on at home,' I blurted out suddenly. 'I was upset about my mum and dad being away so much, and you all seem to think I have such a *great* life because they have so much money. You're always going on about how lucky I am. Well, it's just not like that!'

I saw the other girls look at each other in surprise and concern.

'And I *am* selfish, just like you said,' I rushed on.

'I was walking Chelsea tonight and I saw my friends Flo and Daisy from school, and – and – I was *ashamed* of Chelsea because I'm such a stupid snob, and I tied her up so they wouldn't see her, but when I came back, she was gone!'

I started crying again.

'So why are we standing here wasting time?' Georgie slung her arm around my shoulders and gave me a quick squeeze. 'Let's get searching for Chelsea right away!'

'Shall we split up?' Hannah suggested. 'We can cover a lot of ground more quickly that way.'

Grace nodded. 'Hannah, you and Georgie search the playground,' she said, taking charge in her usual quiet way, 'Katy and Jasmin, you look over by the lake and Lauren and I will carry on looking around here. Is everyone wearing watches?'

We all nodded.

'OK, meet back here in fifteen minutes,' Grace instructed us.

The others immediately ran off. I dried my eyes again, feeling comforted by their obvious concern for me and for Chelsea. But I really *was* an idiot, I knew that now. I'd grown to love Chelsea over the last few weeks, and I hadn't admitted it to myself until right this minute.

'Lauren, why don't you ring home and warn them that Chelsea's lost?' Grace suggested gently. 'Dogs sometimes make their own way back, and it would help if they're looking out for her.'

'OK,' I agreed, taking my phone from my pocket.

Dad answered when I called, and I explained what had happened, getting all tearful again as I did so.

'Oh, Lauren, honey, don't cry,' Dad said, sounding quite upset himself. 'I'm sure we'll find her again. After all, there can't be many dogs who look like Chelsea! Hang on a minute, love…'

There were voices in the background, but I couldn't hear what they were saying. A moment later Dad came back on the line.

'Lauren, your gran's here and she's volunteered to stay in the house in case Chelsea turns up. She's going to keep an eye out for her. Tanya, your mum and I are going to search the streets around here. OK?'

'Thanks, Dad.' I hardly knew how it had happened, but Chelsea had somehow become *everyone's* pet, not just mine. Now all I wanted was to get her back.

Grace and I searched the football field and the surrounding area for a quarter of an hour, but there was no sign of Chelsea. My heart sank like a stone when I saw the others running back to join us, shaking their heads.

'OK, we've covered almost all of the park between us,' Georgie panted. 'I guess we just have to assume that Chelsea has left by one of the gates.'

'But which one?' I asked anxiously. 'It can't be where Chelsea and I came in. I would have seen her come out again while I was talking to Flo and Daisy.'

'Let's try one of the other gates,' Katy suggested.

We hurried through the children's playground to the next set of gates. I tried to block thoughts of Chelsea being knocked over by a car on the busy main road out of my head. But when we reached the gates, there was still no sign of her.

'I think we ought to start searching the streets around the park,' Hannah suggested.

Grace nodded. 'Good idea, Han.'

'Shall we split into twos again?' asked Jasmin.

I was about to reply when suddenly I saw the most *extraordinary* thing. Flo and Daisy were walking towards the park gates. Daisy was carrying Coco in her arms, and Flo had a dog on a lead next to her. The dog was funny and ugly with stumpy little legs.

'CHELSEA!' I screamed, probably loud enough to wake the dead!

Flo and Daisy stared at me in utter amazement as I flew towards them, grinning madly. Chelsea spotted me and lunged forward, almost taking Flo's arm off, her tail wagging like it would never stop. I bent down and gave Chelsea the most enormous hug. She went mad, licking my nose with joy and panting with excitement.

'Lauren, what's going on?' Flo gasped. 'Do you know this dog?'

'Yes,' I declared, taking the lead from her. 'This is Chelsea – and she's *mine*!'

Flo and Daisy gazed at Chelsea and me in disbelief.

'You never told us you had a dog, Lauren!' Daisy said, looking very bewildered. 'We just found her a few minutes ago, wandering around the streets—'

'We thought she might have run out of the park, so Daisy and I decided to bring her back here and see if we could find her owner,' Flo explained. 'If we couldn't, we were going to take her back to Daisy's and ask her mum to call the RSPCA.'

'Well, thanks for bringing her back,' I mumbled. I stared at Daisy and Flo a bit defiantly, *daring* them to say anything mean about Chelsea.

'She's got such a funny, cute little face,' Flo said with a grin, bending to stroke Chelsea's head. I was so shocked, I almost fell over! 'Coco was a bit scared of Chelsea so Daisy had to carry her, but she's very friendly, isn't she?'

'She's a lovely little dog, Lauren,' Daisy chimed in. 'She's got loads of character. I just don't understand why you've never mentioned her before?'

I stared at Flo and Daisy, feeling a bit ashamed of myself. I'd just learnt something I knew I'd never forget in the future – *don't ever assume you know what people think, because they might be thinking the exact opposite!* Flo and Daisy didn't seem to find anything odd about me having a dog like Chelsea.

'Well, I wasn't sure I was keeping her,' I muttered, embarrassed. 'We had to find out if she had another owner, first.'

Suddenly I realised that Hannah, Katy and the others had joined us, and they were all looking a bit bemused. I'd forgotten they'd never met my Riverton friends. 'Oh, guys, these are my mates from school, Flo and Daisy,' I explained quickly.

'They found Chelsea and started looking for her owner. And *these* are my friends from the Springhill Stars...' Quickly I introduced Grace, Georgie, Hannah, Katy and Jasmin.

'Are you into footie?' Georgie asked Flo and Daisy, who both shook their heads.

'Not really,' Flo said, 'Daisy and I go horse-riding, and we do ballet.'

'Lauren came riding with us yesterday,' Daisy added.

Georgie and the others burst out laughing. I grinned too, and so did Flo and Daisy.

'How did Lauren get on?' Grace asked.

'Well—' Daisy began.

'Go on, say it!' I rolled my eyes. 'I was rubbish, wasn't I? And by the way, my bottom's still sore!'

'What about ballet, Lauren?' Katy asked me, a cheeky gleam in her eye. 'Are you going to try that too?'

'Flo and Daisy invited me to go to their dance school with them tomorrow,' I replied, keeping Chelsea close to my side. 'But sorry, you two, I won't be able to come now. I'm going to be playing in the last match of the season for the Springhill Stars instead!'

CHAPTER TWELVE

When I ran out onto the pitch with the rest of the Springhill Stars the following morning, everything in my own little world seemed to be just fine again. Lauren Melissa Bell was back – and how! What a difference to the way I'd felt last week at the game against the Blackbridge Belles... Now I was determined to enjoy the very last game of the season.

One of the *best* things was that I'd made up with the other girls. We were all mates again, and now we were closer than ever. They'd all been shocked when I'd explained in more detail how I'd secretly been so upset about the situation with my mum and dad and Tanya.

'Lauren, you should have said!' Jasmin had burst out, her brow furrowed in concern. 'We *did* think your life was all glossy and perfect and a bit like a celebrity's! Well, I did, anyway.'

'Me too,' Katy added quietly, and Grace, Georgie and Hannah nodded in agreement. 'I'm so sorry, Lauren.'

'We guessed there was something going on with you and Tanya,' Hannah admitted. 'But we just thought you didn't really like her that much. We didn't know you had all this other stuff going on with your mum and dad.'

'I feel bad, now.' Georgie pulled a face at me. 'I wish I hadn't teased you about your parents being so rich, Lauren. Maybe I *was* a bit jealous—'

'Oh, forget it!' I broke in. 'I don't mind being teased. Well, most of the time, anyway. And don't think I'm complaining about my mum and dad having lots of money – I'm not. All I'm saying is that it *doesn't* mean everything's perfect.'

And then there was Chelsea, who was now really and truly *my* dog. I'd phoned home to let everyone know that I'd found her safe and sound. And when we got back, Mum, Dad, Tanya and Gran were all waiting on the doorstep, ready to welcome us.

'I'm not quite sure how it happened,' Gran said thoughtfully as Tanya whisked Chelsea off to the kitchen for a celebratory bowl of minced chicken, 'but that little dog has somehow become part of this family without any of us noticing.'

I nodded. 'I only brought Chelsea home because I wanted to annoy Tanya and make her leave,' I confessed, looking anxiously at Mum and Dad. 'But now I want to keep her.'

'Chelsea or Tanya?' Dad teased.

'Actually – both!' I said with a grin. The war between me and Tanya was now officially over. I was even thinking of asking her if I could email her daughter, Gabriela. It would be fun to have a pen pal in Slovakia!

'I wondered when you'd realise that you were getting so fond of Chelsea, Lauren,' Mum said with a smile. 'I've been seeing this coming for the last week, at least.'

'Your gran's right.' Dad put his arm around me. 'Chelsea's part of the family now. And we'll organise some proper dog-training classes for her – and for you!'

Mum and Dad had also stuck to their promise to try and make things at home better. They'd worked out when they'd both be at home for the next few weeks so that the three of us could have some time together. I was really glad, not just for myself but for Dad, because he looked really tired. He admitted that he'd had some work problems over the last month or so, although he wouldn't tell me and Mum what they were. Too boring, he'd said.

I glanced around the field as we took our positions, ready for kick-off. My mum, dad and Tanya were on the touchline, and we'd even managed to persuade Gran to come along, for once. I don't think she'd been to see me play since I was about *ten*. I hoped no one fouled me, though, because I was a bit nervous of Gran running on and hitting them with her handbag! Dad had Chelsea on her lead, sitting at his feet. He'd promised Freya that he'd make sure she behaved herself.

Freya was standing near them, and she smiled encouragingly at me. She'd told me that she was very relieved that I'd changed my mind about leaving the Stars. Not half as relieved as I was, though!

The ref blew his whistle and the Stars kicked off,

but we lost the ball almost immediately. As I chased back to help out in defence, I saw Flo and Daisy walking across the field towards us along with Mrs Rankin. What a surprise! I came to a dead halt, my mouth falling open.

'Lauren!' Georgie shouted from her goalmouth. 'Stop standing there like a prize prune, and get on with it!'

Yep, everything was back to normal! Katy had won the ball back for us and passed it to Jo-Jo. I dashed off down the field, a little way behind Grace, Hannah, JoJo and Emily, who were sweeping forward with some neat passes. I was still a little behind them when they forced their way into the Tigers' penalty area. Grace took a shot, but the Tigers' goalie pushed it away. The ball rolled through to me and I *belted* it into the net. One–nil! In the first two minutes! Yay, me!

Whooping, Grace and the others ran over to do high fives.

'You're back, Lauren!' Georgie yelled from her goal. 'And you're better than ever!'

Mum, Dad, Tanya, Flo, Daisy and Mrs Rankin were clapping and cheering, and even Gran joined in. Chelsea was barking loudly, but Dad managed to calm her down as, smiling widely, I took my place again, ready for the Tigers to kick off. Everyone I cared about most in the world was right here, right now, and I was doing one of the things I loved most, playing football. I couldn't remember ever feeling happier in my whole life.

Except when I scored another goal in the second half, that is! Grace and Jasmin had already snaffled another two goals before the break, one a header from my cross and one scrambled over the line from a free kick, so my goal meant we went 4–1 up. It was a real team effort too. Georgie stopped an attack by the Tigers and rolled the ball out to Katy. Alicia passed the ball to Jasmin in midfield, who sent it spinning over to Hannah. Hannah to Ruby, Ruby to me, me to Grace. The Tigers didn't get a look-in, and all the time we were moving further and further up the pitch towards their goal.

When we reached the edge of their penalty area, the Tigers tried to close in. But Grace outsmarted them and managed to sweep the ball over to me before she lost it. I went for an instant shot that hit one of the defenders on the legs, but then the ball bounced right back to me. Well, I wasn't going to miss a second time, was I?

'Go, Lauren!' I could hear Georgie yelling from her goal behind me, as I whacked the ball as hard as I could. This time I remembered everything we'd learnt at that intensive training course not long ago, and I *didn't* slice it. The shot stayed low and fast, and I'm telling you, there's no better feeling than when you see the ball beat the goalie and land in the back of the net!

'GOAL!' Georgie and the rest of the Stars yelled. I could hear my mum and dad and Tanya cheering too, and Chelsea was barking excitedly. My gran was almost dancing up and down on the touchline with pride – I'd never seen anything like it!

Then, just before the end, Hannah got a tap-in, laid on by Grace, so we ended up winning the match 5–1, one of our best ever results.

'What a fantastic end to the season!' Georgie crowed, running over to the rest of the team as we hugged each other and jumped up and down with glee in the centre circle.

'You were utterly brilliant, girls.' Freya rushed onto the pitch, looking flushed with pride. 'Now all you've got to do is keep that feeling over the summer, and come back in August, ready to push for promotion!'

'Lauren?' I spun round as I heard Flo calling me from the touchline. 'Sorry, we have to go or we'll be late for ballet class.'

'Thanks for coming!' I called, rushing over to them. 'It was fab to see you here.'

'Well, we've never been to watch you play before, and we were curious,' Daisy admitted with a grin. 'You're much better with a football than you are with a horse, Lauren Bell!'

I laughed. 'Tell the Royal Ballet I'm sorry, but they'll just have to miss out on my dancing talents!' I declared firmly. 'I'm sticking with football.'

Flo and Daisy giggled as they hurried off with Mrs Rankin. Then I ran over to Mum, Dad, Tanya, Gran and Chelsea. Dad swung me off my feet in a bear-hug and I squealed, while Chelsea barked loudly, jumping around us, desperate to be hugged too. When Dad put me down, I picked her up. She was very muddy – but then, so was I!

'Thanks for coming, *all* of you,' I said. But I looked particularly at Gran and at Tanya.

Tanya smiled at me. I still felt a bit ashamed that I'd been mean to her before, but I *had* apologised, and she'd forgiven me. I'd sent my first email to Gabriela too, and I was waiting for a reply. Tanya had been really thrilled that I wanted to write to her daughter.

'Well, Lauren...' Gran seemed at a loss for words. For once! 'All that running around and you're hardly out of breath! And those goals! You really were quite *amazing*—'

I launched myself at her and gave her a huge hug. 'Thanks, Gran. Footie keeps me pretty fit, you know. So –' I grinned innocently at her '– do you think your doctor would approve?'

'Don't be a cheeky madam, Lauren Bell!' But Gran was smiling as she tapped me on the backside with her umbrella. 'Now off you go and get changed before you catch a cold. I think your friends are waiting for you.'

I turned to see Hannah, Georgie, Grace, Jasmin and Katy waiting patiently for me in the centre circle. I'd forgotten how it felt to be so happy, I thought, as I ran over to them. Everything was wonderful again in the mad world of Lauren Melissa Bell! Well, except for Dad looking so tired and worried at the moment. He worked too hard, that was the problem. But I was going to make sure he enjoyed himself with me and Mum when we had our family time.

'Isn't it just *great* the way everything's worked out?' I said happily as I joined the others.

'Oh yes!' Katy agreed. 'Let's make sure we never, ever fall out again. Shall we all promise?'

'Promise!' everyone yelled at the top of their voices.

'And we'll see each other all the time before the beginning of next season, won't we?' Hannah asked.

'You bet!' Grace said confidently. 'We'll miss playing football *loads,* but we can meet up every week and have a kick-around in the park.'

'And it's my birthday in July, just before the summer holidays,' I added. 'My mum and dad have promised me the best surprise birthday celebration *ever*, and you lot are all invited. They won't tell me what they're planning – but it's something to do with *football!*'

'Wow!' Jasmin's eyes opened wide. 'That sounds *sooo* exciting!'

'Hey, you know what I just realised?' Georgie grinned round at the others. 'It's FUN being mates with someone who's mega-rich!'

I gave her a friendly shove. Then we all grabbed each other's hands and we hurtled towards the changing-rooms in a long line, dragging each other along and shrieking with laughter as we ran.

How could I ever *have given this up?* I asked myself. I was back with my mates in the Springhill Stars, and that was where I was going to stay!

WIN £50 TOPSHOP VOUCHERS!

Just answer the following questions:

1. What does Lauren name her dog?
2. Lauren's bedroom is decorated in which two colours?
3. What was the score in the Stars' final match against Turnwood Tigers?

Log on to

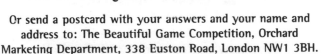

www.thebeautifulgamebooks.co.uk

NOW for your chance to win!

Or send a postcard with your answers and your name and address to: The Beautiful Game Competition, Orchard Marketing Department, 338 Euston Road, London NW1 3BH.

Full terms and conditions are available online.
Competition closes 31st March 2010.

THE BEAUTIFUL GAME

Have you read the first book in the series?

Five new mates, plenty of football –
Hannah should feel like a champion.
But what about her BIG SECRET?

THE BEAUTIFUL GAME

Can't get enough of Lauren and her friends?

Here's a taster of book 3 –

GEORGIE'S WAR

CHAPTER ONE

"Luke! Get *off* me!" I roared, kicking my arms and legs furiously. I was being pinned down on the sofa by my idiot brother, and he was piling cushions on top of me.

"Give in, then, and tell me where it is!" Luke yelled. He chucked another cushion on top of the heap, and then leaned heavily on them so that I couldn't get up. His face was bright red, and his long black hair was sticking up and out all over the place. Luke always thinks he's *so* cool with his millions of girlfriends – wouldn't it be funny if one of them could see him right now?

"NO!" Gritting my teeth, I managed to fight my

way up through the barrier of cushions. I gave Luke a shove he wasn't expecting, and he went staggering backwards across the living room. "You're not having it!"

"OW!" Luke hit his toe on the coffee table and gave a loud, dramatic groan. Honestly, what *is* it with men and pain? They always have to make a big deal of it – and I should know, living with three brothers and a dad. If they get a sniffle, it's, like, a major health crisis. No wonder it's women who have babies. Men would *never* be able to cope with *that*!

I giggled at the look on Luke's face, and he glared at me.

"I'm telling Dad!" he burst out.

"We interrupt this argument to bring you an important piece of world-breaking news," I said in my best, annoying, American accent. "*Luke Tells Dad!*"

Luke's eyes narrowed. "Right, give me that remote control this minute, Georgie, or you're deader than the deadest thing in the entire universe!" he shouted.

"Tough!" I retorted, "*I* was here first, and *I* want to watch *The Vampire Chronicles*!"

I settled myself down on the sofa again next to Rainbow, our black cat. Rainbow hadn't moved an inch while Luke was trying to smother me with cushions. In fact, he hadn't even opened his eyes.

Rainbow was pretty old now – my mum had found him starving in the street fifteen years ago, when my brother Jack was still a baby, and had brought him home. Rainbow was a bit deaf now, which probably wasn't a bad thing, living in this house.

Luke frowned. Then he spun round and switched the TV off, turning back to grin annoyingly at me.

"Put the TV on!" I howled.

Luke folded his arms. "Make me."

Fuming, I flew across the room just as the door opened. Dad walked in, and I crashed straight into him.

"OOF!" Dad gasped, as I knocked the breath out of him. "What's going on in here? It sounds like World War Three."

Luke and I both began yelling at the same time.

"*I* want to watch *The Vampire Chronicles*!" I shrieked.

"Well, *I* want to watch a documentary about space travel!" Luke roared. "It's for school," he added, glancing virtuously at Dad.

"Oh, please!" I snapped. "You mean you want to see *Sun and Fun in Ibiza*, so that you can drool over girls in bikinis –"

"STOP!" Dad yelled, sticking his fingers in his ears. "This is why you both have TVs in your bedrooms."

"But I want to watch the big flat-screen in here," Luke and I whined at exactly the same moment. I don't know why we argue so much. Maybe it's because Luke is only two years older than I am. But I honestly don't remember us fighting this much before Mum died...

"What will it take for you two to get along a bit better?" Dad went on, raising his eyes to heaven. "I wish I knew!" Poor old Dad, he seems to be getting more and more fed up every day with all the rows. "Luke, go and do your homework. Georgie, go and get ready for football training. Adey's going to drop you off at the college." He held up his hand as Luke and I both opened our mouths again. "No, I *really* don't want to hear it. I've had a hard day at the office. Now get out of here, the pair of you."

Luke stalked off, looking deeply annoyed. I scooted after him, secretly wondering if I could trip him up in the hall and then get to the safety of my bedroom before he caught me. On the other hand, maybe I'd let him off this time, I decided. I was *much* more excited about getting ready for the first training session of the new season. I couldn't *wait* to see the other girls. Well, I'd seen Hannah, Grace and Katy at school today, and all six of us had got together at least once every week since the season finished. Lauren had had her birthday in May, and her parents, who are *seriously* loaded, booked a day at a Brazilian soccer school for the six of us. It was a great laugh. You wouldn't *believe* the tricks we can all do with a football now!

We'd also met up with Freya Reynolds, our *fantabulous* coach, a few times too. Mr and Mrs Fleetwood, Hannah's parents, had had a barbeque in their back garden during the summer holidays, and they'd invited Freya as well as us girls and our parents. It had been big fun, even though Olivia, Hannah's snooty half-sister, had ignored us!

But nothing could beat the excitement of us all getting together at our VERY FIRST training session of the season. That was beyond special. The Springhill Stars Under-13s team was back in business. YAY! And I just *knew* we were going to get promotion to the top league this season, I could feel it in my bones—

"Georgie?"

I turned back as I reached the door.

"Yes, Dad?"

"Where's the remote control?" asked Dad, the ghost of a twinkle in his eye.

I went over to the sofa and stuck my hand between Rainbow and the cushion. Rainbow gave a sleepy chirrup as I pulled out the remote control from underneath his fluffy tail.

"Thank you," Dad said.

I left him watching the news and went upstairs. Luke had vanished into his room, sulking probably, but Jack was coming down as I went up.

"What's happening, Fishface?" he said, giving me a punch on the shoulder.

"Ow," I said automatically, even though it didn't really hurt. "Don't do that, Ugly Mug."

Jack tried to punch me again, but this time I slapped his hand away. We wrestled for a bit, trying to push each other down the stairs (don't panic, we were only a few steps up). Then Dad came out of the living-room and told us to be quiet, he couldn't hear the TV.

Jack and I get on slightly better than Luke and me, but not *that* much, to be honest with you. Jack's sixteen, two years older than Luke, but they're good mates, so Jack usually takes his side. They both tease me and try to boss me around, but I don't put up with any of their garbage. I stand up for myself and speak out. I have to, otherwise my voice would just get lost in the all-male crowd in this house.

I shoved my way past Jack, ran upstairs and burst into my bedroom, humming the theme tune from *Match of the Day*. There I threw off my school uniform and dragged my Spurs shirt and a pair of navy trackie bottoms out of my wardrobe. It was early September but the weather was still quite warm, so I grabbed an old denim jacket that used to belong to Dad, and slung it on over the top. That would do fine. Then I scraped back my masses of black, curly hair and held it off my face with a black stretchy headband that had *definitely* seen better days.

You've probably guessed by now that you're unlikely to see me in the front row of the audience at London Fashion Week! Honestly, I just can't be *bothered* with all that girlie stuff. Grace asked me once if I'd always been a tomboy, or if I act this way because I want to be like my brothers. I didn't know what to say. I *thought* I'd always been like this, but I remember loving to watch my mum putting on her make-up and helping her choose what to wear, when I was a little girl...

But anyway, I'd never hear the end of it from Luke and Jack if I went all glam and girlie now. They'd laugh their heads off. I couldn't be doing with that.

I took my purple Springhill Stars shirt and put it carefully in my sports bag, along with my white shorts. Freya doesn't mind if we don't wear our match kits for training, but it's become a tradition that we all wear them at the very first session of the new season. It kind of *reminds* us how important the team is, and gets us off to a great start.

Thinking of Freya reminded me that I had

something to ask her. I took my battered old mobile out of my pocket and rattled out a text message.

Hi, Freya, can I talk to u after training 2nite?

A reply came whizzing back about two seconds later.

Sure! C u soon, F.

Smiling, I slipped my phone back into my pocket. I'd been playing for the Stars ever since I was eight years old. Freya was my coach for that first season, then, as I'd got older and moved into different teams – Under-10s, Under-11s and so on – I'd had other coaches. But Freya was the one I liked the most, so I was dead pleased when she took over the Under-13s. She'd been really kind to me when my mum died.

Freya was straight down the line. You always knew where you stood with her. And she's so cool. She rides a motorbike, a huge big shiny thing! I think she's great, even though we've had some fierce run-ins over the years...

About the Author

Narinder Dhami lives in Cambridge with her husband Robert and their three cats, but was originally born in Wolverhampton. Her dad came over from India in 1954, and met and married her mum, who is English. Narinder always wanted to write, but after university taught in London for ten years before becoming a writer.

For the last thirteen years Narinder has been a full-time author. She has written over 100 children's books, as well as many short stories and articles for children's magazines. *Lauren's Best Friend* is the second book in The Beautiful Game series.

Since her childhood, Narinder has been a huge football fan.